THE ARCHERS OF AMBRIDGE

THE ARCHERS OF AMBRIDGE

By

GEOFFREY WEBB

AND

EDWARD J. MASON

By arrangement with the B.B.C.

LONDON

GEORGE NEWNES LIMITED

TOWER HOUSE, SOUTHAMPTON STREET

STRAND, W.C.2

First published 1954
Second impression 1954
Third impression 1954
Fourth impression 1954
Fifth impression 1955

MADE AND PRINTED IN GREAT BRITAIN BY PURNELL AND SONS, LTD.
PAULTON (SOMERSET) AND LONDON

I

OVER the Atlantic a strong west wind was saving the petrol and the engines, so that the crew and the thirty passengers of the aircraft could whisper and be heard above the muted throb of power.

Almost unnoticed by the dozing passengers, the night had faded and black had turned to grey. They were moving into the dawn as they flew towards England. Below them was a ship, and seamen on watch noted the passage of the plane for the few moments that it was overhead.

The ship was a freighter laden with tinned fruit and wheat from Canada for the mills and shops of Great Britain. The rich harvests of the great plains of Saskatchewan were being carried across the wide ocean, yet to the crew it was merely another routine voyage.

To the watching business man in the aircraft above, however, there was nothing routine about transport. His mind, alert even at that early hour, had probed the shape and direction of the ship. He could be reasonably certain that she carried grain for Liverpool. He wondered what she would carry back to Canada—machinery, perhaps, or woollen cloth, or the delicate china of Staffordshire.

Trade was nectar and ambrosia to Henry Crawford. Columns of statistics showing a balance of trade affected him as wine affected other men. He could slake his thirst for power on the sight of bills of lading neatly docketed in his briefcase. He would go without food rather than miss a directors' meeting. All the boards of which he was a member were soundly prosperous because of his uncanny ability to make money.

Around him in the aircraft other passengers were beginning to stir. Opposite was a Canadian honeymoon couple; in front of the newly-weds a middle-aged man who seemed to be a transatlantic equivalent of Henry Crawford.

This was Cyrus J. Standish, who wore hand-made shoes, a heavy grey gaberdine suit, a red-and-white tie, rimless spectacles and a soft felt hat.

Watching him, Crawford wondered about Standish —not whether anybody loved him, whether he kept a dog and gardened, where he went for his holidays or of what secret he might be ashamed; Crawford was trying to place him in the right trade. He decided that Standish was in the motor business, and that his briefcase contained folders about new cars and tractors.

But Crawford was wrong, as he was so often wrong about people. They were not his medium of expression. He could push goods about, transfer machines from one town to another, transmute raw materials to quality goods for sale, but sometimes he was thwarted by an exasperating human element he was unable to control. In Canada, for example, he had spoken to a board about the vast possibilities of aluminium. He promised increased outlets in industry —more aluminium furniture, machines, light parts for cars, roofing, piping, containers and plumbing parts; all he wanted in return was a thousand shares in the company. The directors knew that he was a man of his word, well able to implement his promise to open

6

up new markets; but something had gone wrong. The chairman, without any reason to show for it, had not liked Crawford, and because of that simple, exasperating, incalculable factor, Crawford's trip to Canada had been a failure and he had not been elected to the board.

The sky was pearling into light, with a faint blush of day ahead, when Cyrus J. Standish leaned forward, his mild eyes half open. He too had looked at the ship below, but for him the wheat had recalled Iowa and the small university where he taught.

He thought about the people who would eat the flour—dock-workers in Glasgow and mill-hands in Rochdale, perhaps. Did any of them, as they cut their morning sandwiches, ever think of the farmers a hemisphere away, who enabled them to eat?

The sky was almost transparent, a great globe of softest rose encompassing the aircraft, not dwarfing it, but making it part of a greater magnificence. Below was a frill of dainty white, a tiny picture of wild waves hammering at the hard coast of Cornwall. Darkly green glowered the fields, while the rose sky reflected the white scars on the soil.

Henry Crawford's mind had fastened on those white scars. Cornish clay was worth investigating, he thought. He had been told a year ago over a drink in a pub—and he never forgot anything—that some of the Cornish mines had closed for lack of capital. He knew the Potteries and their insatiable needs. When he had finished with that trifling matter of ironstone, it might be worth his while to go down to Cornwall and have a look at the clay situation.

To Cyrus J. Standish, who had gained his considerable knowledge of England from books, that glimpse of Cornwall brought to mind King Arthur and the gallant fight of his minority against change. He wanted to go down there and see what had happened to the descendants of the Ancient Britons, the small, quick-witted, dark-eyed, imaginative people who had, in the long ago, fought the invaders and almost won.

He stood up and turned round, stretching his arms above his head, looking at Crawford incidentally.

"There," thought Cyrus, who always attributed the best to people, "is the backbone of England, a man of his word, not flamboyant, never taking unnecessary risks, keeping himself prosperous, but making his country prosperous too."

Then, yawning, he went down to shave.

Crawford rubbed his bristly jaw reflectively. Not long now to Heath Row, where his wife would meet him with the car. She was always efficient—why else had he married her?—and she had doubtless remembered to bring him freshly pressed clothes. He would wash and shave at the airport, change, and then drive on to the Midlands for his next business while his wife went home by bus. Better spend the time now going over the papers—a speed-up in the manufacture of spare parts for machinery, new lorries for the subsidiary firm, an investigation into carelessness in a packing concern, which seemed to have lost a consignment of toys for India.

And there was the matter of ironstone at Ambridge.

Cyrus came back and sat down, inclining his fairish, greying head to the window. His briefcase with its slim books of poetry rested lightly on his knee. There was a port below—Portsmouth, he thought. Pity he had missed Plymouth, with its reminder of his own

8

ancestors. He wondered how many eager Americans, like himself, were coming for a kind of pilgrimage to the places they knew so well by repute. Perhaps not many at this time of year. Then the sea was lost, and the land lay patterned below, gold and brown and richly green, criss-crossed by wandering white lanes, occasionally bisected by arterial roads, now flecked with traffic. Where were all those people going this bright October morning? Cyrus wondered.

"Fasten your safety belts, please," said the air hostess.

As the plane flew over the clustered suburbs of Greater London, Cyrus became excited. His trip would begin in a few minutes. Boy, to see King Charles I's statue in Whitehall, plays at Stratford, the very house in the Chilterns where Milton wrote *Paradise Lost*!

The plane wheeled, circled, circled again, and came smoothly in to land.

"This is England—England!" thought Cyrus excitedly as his feet touched the tarmac. "The England of Shakespeare, the green and pleasant land of Blake! Boy, am I going to love every minute of this!"

Henry Crawford let his wife kiss him.

"Have a good trip?" she asked anxiously. She always asked that.

"Not too bad," he replied, as he always replied.

They chatted desultorily over their coffee, not noticing Cyrus in the corner, watching them, wondering to himself, "Has he really *looked* at her these last ten years?"

But Crawford had no time to look—he never had. Before long he was in his car driving through the hills into Oxfordshire, which meant dreaming spires to people like Standish, but atoms and motor cars to Crawford.

He spent a couple of hours at a factory and then headed the car farther north. The engine purred contentedly and Crawford noticed little of the countryside through which he passed. The limits of his interest were the grey stone walls, the blackthorn hedges and elms flanking the road. Had he bothered to look on either side of him, he would have seen rich agricultural country, good pastures and yellow stubbles as a reminder of the season's crop. Herds of sheep and cows, well-filled and sturdy after the summer's lush grazing, waited for the first chill of winter and fed quietly, an occasional head raised at the passing of Crawford's car.

Good flat country, easily worked and well-stocked, prosperous enough to support the people who kept it in good heart.

Crawford was aware that the road dipped through a fold in the hills only because he had to change down at a nasty bend. Before him in the valley, under a haze of smoke, was the city of Borchester, its ribbon-built suburbs reaching out like probing fingers from the cathedral and county hall into the surrounding countryside.

The car was soon caught up in the stream of traffic through the narrow streets of the town, where seemingly all roads led down to the Industrial Hotel.

Crawford went into the hotel for a late lunch with a business friend. As they began their meal, a man at the next table called for his bill.

He went out, and Crawford's friend said, "That's Lawson-Hope. Has a lot of influence in Ambridge."

With his mouth full, Crawford replied, "Not much influence for good, if he's as unbusinesslike as his cousin Colonel Percy. Think he might be sticky?"

"No," said the other man. "He's broke, expects to keep up an estate without applying real business sense to it. Thinks the honour and glory of being squire is quite enough to set him apart from us lesser mortals. When you want anything from him, just talk to him of hunting and shooting and probably the silly old blighter will eat out of your hand."

"Thanks, old man," said Crawford.

Lawson-Hope stood on the pavement outside the Industrial Hotel thinking hard, trying to remember where he had left his car. Although he had been coming to Borchester for as long as he could remember, his sense of direction always deserted him.

He wandered vaguely, hopefully, down towards Cathedral Square, reflecting that cities were no place for him. He seemed to remember leaving the car outside the saddler's shop, but could not be sure.

Eventually he discovered it in the cathedral car-park and drove slowly through a maze of scurrying traffic. The air was thick with petrol and oil fumes, which always made him feel short-tempered. Beyond the outer suburbs, he knew, the air was clear and sweet and clean; here it was filled with poison from factories, engines and cars.

As he drove he glanced about him.

In the cars were fleshy men like that dark fellow he had glimpsed in the hotel. The women looked decent enough—but he admitted to himself that he was not too critical a judge of women. Horseflesh was a different matter.

He slowed near a bus-stop, glancing at a line of laughing, brightly-dressed factory girls. He liked them too. But behind them stood a girl who was not laughing—a country girl he recognised.

He drew his car in to the pavement. "Hello, Christine."

"Afternoon, Squire," said Christine Archer. She moved a pile of parcels from one aching arm to the other.

"Going home?" he asked.

"Yes. I'm just waiting for the Ambridge bus."

"Hop in, then. I'll take you."

"Are you sure?" asked Christine dubiously. "I don't want to trouble you."

"Not at all, not at all," said Lawson-Hope. "Hop in. Just wait a moment while I shift these parcels to the back." He moved his new fishing-rods quickly, fumbling a little because a bus was hooting indignantly behind them.

Christine, blushing slightly at the speculative stares of the girls in the bus queue, sat stiffly beside him, her parcels piled on her knee.

Just outside the city he pulled up.

"Let's put them all in the back, shall we?"

Lawson-Hope put all her parcels in the back for her, and asked, "What's in the parcels? Or is it a secret?"

"No secret," she said, as the car started moving again. "My brother Phil said—well—he told me to come into Borchester and—well, he said, 'For God's sake, girl, get yourself some new clothes.'"

"Brothers can be beastly," said Lawson-Hope sympathetically.

"Oh no, sir, it wasn't like that at all. He gave me the money himself. No one could have a nicer brother!"

"Fine fellow," said the Squire amiably. He was in a better mood now that he could see green about him and soft blue above.

He looked sideways at Christine, noting the sensible brogues, the green Harris tweed suit, the pale lemon blouse and collar, her soft complexion and the remarkable fairness of her thick hair. She was a nice-looking lass, and would make some young farmer a comely wife.

The car turned right through the edge of Pulcombe Wood. It had the reputation of being always good for a fox, although Lawson-Hope had never hunted it.

"Tell me, Christine, have you read *As You Like It?*" The Squire had often fancied himself as a philosophical Jacques, amongst the stones and running brooks.

"Yes, I have."

"And what did you think of it?"

"I thought they must have got awfully cold out there in the forest sometimes," Christine grinned.

The Squire smiled at her practicality and resolved that for the time being he would not bore her with philosophy.

He turned his car to the right through Felpersham, towards his home.

"It was lucky for me you turned up, wasn't it?" she said.

"Not excessively strange. I always go slowly past that bus-stop—there's usually someone from Ambridge."

"What I meant was, we all thought you'd gone to London."

"I was down there with my wife until yesterday. She will be back in Ambridge in a few days. Some feminine fripperies caught her eye and she had to stay to buy them."

He smiled, including Christine, his wife and the rest of their sex in one vast mystery. There was something about him, Christine thought, that always made her feel important. It was not hard to imagine the long-ago generations of Lawson-Hopes, chivalrous in armour or in velvet and lace, making every woman feel like a princess.

"You are fortunate," he said, "none of you women have to worry about work and the rates—only about spending money."

Christine did not reply. She hoped he had not noticed her hardened hands.

"And how blissful it is to be young!" he went on. "Young, with the world at your feet, able to reach out and have anything you want. You're like that—and so is my niece Jacqueline and that red-haired poultry girl and that lovely dark daughter of Fairbrother's. At this moment, I suppose, she hasn't a thought except for what frock she will choose for the next ball. Lucky Miss Fairbrother!"

Christine, who knew otherwise, still did not reply.

Grace Fairbrother stood in the rose garden at the front of the farmhouse while a redwing flew over her home. With her face upturned, she watched the bird circle for a moment. She wished that she could identify herself with it, losing all her complexities and imperfections in the uncaring joy of a creature on the wing, dipping from the sun into the dark of a tree and going out again without thought into the bright gold above.

At last it flew down, exhausted by its long flight across the ocean, and perched in a tree by the gate, preening itself in the pale October sun. First one feather then another was flaunted; then the wings folded to the bird's side and the girl watched, envious of its uncaring self-satisfaction.

To Grace, the bird in its pride was a poignant reminder by contrast of her own unhappiness. Her short and shining hair accentuated the drawn pallor of her cheeks. Weighed down with a feeling of loneliness that she could not comfort unaided, she walked quickly through the gate and across the gravel drive that led into the farmyard in search of the only person whose affection was strong enough to bring her the solace she needed.

When she saw Phil Archer he was standing outside the farm office, hands deep in the fobs of his whipcord breeches. The sun caught his broad forehead and the wisp of fair curl that always resisted his efforts to push it back out of the way. The quiet, wide-apart grey eyes that gave serenity to his face were not looking in Grace's direction; they were studying the features of the young poultry girl in rough breeches and jersey who was saying something to him that claimed his attention.

To Grace, town-bred, possibly over-sophisticated, there was a wholesome appeal about the simplicity and strength of Phil Archer. Sensitive, inclined to worry and to imagine overmuch, she had, in the past, been able to take her troubles and fears to him, content to wait until his quiet and sensible appraisement of her problems had taught her to face them wisely and well.

At the sight of him, Grace felt a momentary lightening of her spirits, and she waved a greeting. The discussion between Phil and the girl stopped; they turned towards her, and she waited for them to call her.

In their bearing she saw the same aloofness she had come to recognise all too often lately in the village of Ambridge. From Phil it was almost too galling to endure.

When they did not speak she passed by as II intent on going to the stables, which were almost opposite the office across the farmyard. She could feel them watching her and her sense of isolation increased.

"Phil," she thought to herself. "Phil—not you, too!" The only man on whom she thought she could rely seemed to have taken sides—against her.

She collected her horse from the stables, mounted, and without looking at Phil clattered through the yard and down the gravel drive to the turf of the pasture near the square, Georgian farmhouse. There she set the horse up the slopes of her father's fields towards the gaunt drilling equipment outlined against the misty sky.

She was growing to hate that drill, which reminded her of how things had changed during the few short weeks the mineralogist and his technicians had been among them. Before that she and Phil were happy, secure in their love for each other. Now she wondered if things would ever be the same again.

The drill was not so much sinister in itself as in what it represented. Far away beyond it was the faint, unhealthy smudge in the sky which was always associated with industry. There, in Felpersham, men had been torn from their roots. They lived divorced from nature and from the dignity of the land. The drill immediately before her brought industry terrifyingly near. The values of Ambridge were as old as man's first discovery of the soil: the values the drill symbolised were harsh, new and disastrous for the peace of Ambridge.

Grace rode past it with her head averted, saw her father a couple of fields away and cantered to overtake him.

"Daddy, wait!" she called. "Please wait. I must talk to you. It's terribly important."

Fairbrother turned, head on one side, hands behind his back. He was in his middle forties and there was a fastidious neatness about his whole appearance which gave the impression that although he owned the three-hundred-acre farm he could never quite shake off the atmosphere of his original environment, the city. There was none of the ruddiness of the countryman in his pale face, which had the well-scrubbed unwrinkled look of a typical business man.

In the time they had lived here, Grace had watched her father changing. He had lost the tense, suspicious look of the city business man; he had learnt to reflect and consider. But since the drill had stood in his fields his newly-gained values had seemed to drop away from him.

Grace dismounted. Her head came up only to his shoulder and she had to stand back as she spoke in order that he could see her face.

"Everyone's turned against us, Daddy, everybody. Even people I thought couldn't be shaken by a thing like this. All Ambridge is cool."

"Nonsense." He smiled at her. "You're over-sensitive."

"I'm not, I'm not!" She began to grow annoyed with herself for her inability to convince him. "Every time I come through the village it's there—in the way people look and speak. Suspicion, resentment, dislike —they're all there, Daddy, I assure you."

"Imagination," he said tolerantly. His voice had the same softness he had used in the old days to staff who came to him with exaggerated reports of office quarrels.

She wanted to believe him, but she knew that it was useless to try to fool herself.

"You don't want to listen to me. You're determined not to. But I—I'm afraid of what might happen if you go through with this scheme. Can't you ring up that man Crawford and tell him not to come?"

"My dear little Grace, let's be practical."

That was the keyword of his life. He was a sensible, balanced man, given neither to taking risks nor to considering sentiment.

"Practical!" she echoed scornfully.

"The country's badly in need of steel and there's ten million tons of ironstone under our land here and on the Manor estate. The only practical thing to do is to mine it."

"It isn't!" She wished he wouldn't be so positive. "Don't you see—it isn't practical because Ambridge people don't want it. They resent it—and us."

"It's not the mining they resent, it's change—any kind of upset. They'll come round to my way of thinking once they've got used to the idea—especially when they realise they'll profit by it."

Grace shook her head. What profit would it be to the people of Ambridge to get money and lose their traditional livelihood? To them, the principal use of money had always been to buy equipment to improve their farms. Money spent on the land was a living thing, like young crops, but money in their hands and pockets would be dead and meaningless.

Fairbrother absently-mindedly kissed her forehead.

"You go off for your ride and don't worry your head about it," he said. "Subjects like mining shouldn't interest pretty girls. Just enjoy yourself."

He never realised how much he hurt her by these cheerful dismissals, by his refusal to admit she was mature and capable of forming judgments. She knew it gave him pleasure to lavish affection on her, but to him she hadn't grown up. She was still a child, a plaything, something to be amused and entertained and soothed but never taken quite seriously.

She mounted, feeling lonelier than ever.

"Go and have a look at the drill," he called after her. "Jolly interesting. Get the mineralogist to explain how it works."

No! *That* least of all!

Instead she rode to a point where she could look across the shallow valley towards the village. Below her and beyond the meadows where her father's pedigree Ayrshires were grazing, she could see the squat, broad figure of the Squire's gamekeeper cutting the reeds where the trout stream bent sharply after emerging from the wood.

A countryman doing the job of the countryside, she thought. Keeping things in order—like farmers did. What if they were figures of fun in music halls? What if they did appear ungainly in town or made up an uncomprehending audience at a modern play? Every farmer, she believed, was at heart an artist, expressing his deep love of the soil in the contour of the fields and the spacious p nting of wide and lovely trees. The country around Ambridge was a work of art that was a memorial to ll the generations of patient men who had shaped an l moulded it so that utility and beauty would combine for the benefit of generations to come.

And now someone—her father—wanted to change all that.

The pattern of the fields beyond her father's land stretched on past the line of trees to where the road transversed the opposite slope. There, half hidden by an old tithe barn and the sheds at right angles to it, stood a mellow stone farmhouse—Brookfield, Phil's home.

There had been friendship for her at Brookfield long before the Fairbrothers were generally accepted as part of the life of Ambridge. When she was a stranger in this conservative society, the Archers helped bridge the gap that somehow set her apart from the villagers. She tried not to think of the look on Phil's face just now, but made herself remember the warmth and kindly understanding of his parents, Dan and Doris, and his sister, Christine.

Those memories made her nudge her mount down the slope towards the farm. Perhaps at Brookfield they would understand her divided loyalties. She reined in twice before she covered a hundred yards, nervous of going on to discover the truth for herself.

But the horse knew its way. It had travelled the route many times in the past when things had been so different. She let the reins go slack in her hands and the horse took over.

II

THROUGH all his years of farming—thirty of them as tenant of Brookfield itself—Dan Archer never came across a job that tried his patience so much as teaching a calf to drink from a pail.

The calf he was handling in the gloom of one of the sheds off the farmyard was no different from dozens of others he had reared in his time.

"Wayward as they make 'em. Come on, you daft ha'porth. You don't want to starve, do you?"

He was bent over, a tilted bucket of milk clenched between his shins. One hand rested in the warm milk while the other guided the calf's gangling head into the bucket. He encouraged it to suck at his half-submerged fingers, easing its mouth deeper into the milk as it did so.

"Will Fairbrother go through with it, d'you think?"

Dan looked up at the sound of his wife's quiet voice and was in time to see the dimples in her elbows disappear when she bent her bare plump arms to lean on top of the half-door.

"Seems determined enough. Can't understand the chap." The calf gave a skittish jerk of its head and tilted the bucket. A creamy pool trickled through the strawed floor and under the door, out into the yard. Dan adjusted the pail, endured his aching back and then roused the calf's interest in his fingers again.

"There's good, rich farming land across there," his level voice came out of the gloom. "It didn't get that way by accident either. It's in good heart because in the past people had the sense to take care of it and put back into the soil what they took out of it. Why wreck all that with opencast mining?"

The bucket clanked noisily and the calf scuttled back a couple of paces. It planted its forelegs wide, knock-kneed, unstable, impishly defiant. It had to be hauled back to its feed, which it suddenly started to take voraciously.

"Thank heaven this ironstone business doesn't affect our land, Dan," Doris said. Though they had been married for thirty years, they had never failed to discuss their daily problems with a mutual common-sense and frankness that made trouble easier to confront.

"Our land seems safe enough, but if the ironstone scheme comes off it'll be a different Ambridge. And I don't think I'll like it."

Everything had happened very quickly. A few weeks back young Bill Slater, one of Dan's two employees, had been trying out a new tractor and had crashed into an outcrop of rock on Fairbrother's land. Fairbrother discovered it was ironstone and had asked a mineralogist in to survey the extent of the ironfield. Blasting and drilling established that it spread under Fairbrother's land and the greater part of the Manor estate, most of which was broken up into tenant farms on both sides of the river. It involved hundreds of acres, an irregular blot on the mineralogist's map that took no account of traditions or boundary fences.

Dan spoke again, quietly and thoughtfully.

"If they fetch in their blessed cranes and grabs and bulldozers they'll make the place unrecognisable, and when they've finished Lord alone knows how long it'll take to get the land back into shape again. Maybe not in our lifetime. Why couldn't they have found the stuff at Borchester, under the Town Hall?"

"Squire'll never let the estate be pulled about like that," Doris said with more confidence than she felt. It was no secret that the Squire had been hard put in recent years to keep the estate together and might well be tempted to accept the scheme for the income it would bring. For the last twenty years landowners throughout England had been forced to sell because of tax and duty. Why should Ambridge expect to escape? She went on doubtfully:

"I wish he hadn't been away, because nobody can be quite sure. I hope he says 'No' firmly when he comes back. The whole thing's had a terrible effect in the village. People are unhappy—uneasy. There's even quarrelling within families."

"Small wonder." Again Dan's fingers patiently coaxed the calf to the milk.

"Simon was grousing at Bill this morning for turning up the ironstone in the first place. That's your own two men pulling against each other." She glanced over her shoulder to Fairbrother's house, just visible between the trees of the orchard. "It's bad for our Phil, too. He's upset."

"So would you be if you got a job as farm manager and just after you'd got the place running nicely your gaffer came and told you he was going to turn it upside down."

"It's weeks since Grace was here," she said thoughtfully. "She must know what people in the village are saying and thinking. We're a part of Ambridge and I suppose she thinks we feel the same."

Eventually, in spite of itself, the calf drank its fill. Dan straightened himself to his full six feet and ducked out of the gloom of the shed. In build he was well-made, straight-backed, with no surplus flesh on him. His iron-grey hair, receding a little from the forehead, was revealed for a few moments as he lifted and resettled his battered trilby. He was ruddy-complexioned and the high, firm cheekbones and a close-clipped, square, grey moustache did not hide a pleasantly formed mouth that more often than not looked ready to smile.

"I don't think I could ever leave here and there's nothing I'd ever want changed," Doris said mournfully.

They stood together for a few moments, he in his old check jacket, dungarees and gumboots, she in her house-frock and large comfortable apron, remembering their thirty-odd years of married life at Brookfield. On this farm they had raised two sons and a daughter. The years had always seemed busy and wisely spent, filled with activity and companionship. But the changes they had seen together were all natural changes—the mellowing and renaissance of the seasons, the rhythm of planting and harvest, the maturing of their children, the deeper and closer dependence on each other as they aged. Each change had been foreseen, but this new change would be something that could destroy their life-work and rob them of their home and their individuality.

Dan set down the pail, wiped his hand across his thigh and reached for his pipe, musing that there were a great many jobs to be done to keep a hundred-acre farm going. Because he *would* keep it going, right to the end.

She might have been reading his thoughts.

"You'll have to get Simon or Bill to clean up the yard a bit, once the ploughing is done. Disinfectant wouldn't do it much harm. And must you keep that old ploughshare of your grandfather's? And can't you find some use for three leaking rusty buckets that you won't let me throw away?"

"Ay—though we can't do everything at once, love. I think I'll just go down to see how they're getting on with pulling and topping the sugar beet, then I'm going on to shift the electric fence in the kale."

"Wait." She saw the Squire's car approaching, nudged her husband, and nodded in the direction of the road. "Find out what you can. Tell him everybody in the village is depending on him."

Dan nodded and walked over to the yard gate to greet the tall, military-looking figure just emerging from the car. Christine jumped out with her parcels, thanked the Squire and ran across to where Doris stood.

"Afternoon, Squire. Didn't know you were home. Glad to see you back." Dan leaned on the gate, preparing for a long talk. "Thanks for giving Christine a lift."

Arthur Clive Lawson-Hope's responsive smile brought an intricate pattern of wrinkles around his sunken eyes, over which the bushy eyebrows jutted like twisted wool. The wrong side of sixty, he had a long face and drooping cheeks. The slight stoop of his shoulders was accentuated by the almost Edwardian cut of his tweeds, but he still walked and stood well. The Squire of Ambridge did not regard himself as an old man. Field sports were still his major interest, and anything that interfered with his shooting and hunting was given short shrift.

He raised his hat to Doris, who had joined them with Christine. It was not long before explanations were forthcoming.

"Fairbrother rang me up about three weeks ago just as my wife and I were hurrying off to London and asked me if I'd mind some surveying being done on the estate," the squire said in his matter-of-fact, practical tone. "Naturally I told him to go ahead. I'd no idea what was involved until he rang me last night to report on the result." He shook his head slowly. "Incredible fellow. Quite extraordinary. Not unlike a bulldozer. Wants to go into partnership with me, and mine the stuff. So far as he's concerned it's quite straightforward. I've got the land, he's got the money. It's as simple as that—or so he thinks."

"I'm afraid the village is up in arms at the thought of it," Dan said. "The farmers on the estate especially."

"They needn't worry, Mr. Archer. As I told Fairbrother, I like Ambridge as it is." He nodded slowly, as though he mentally checked his statements and confirmed them. "But here's a point. I don't own the mineral rights. They're held by my cousin out in Kenya. You probably remember him—Colonel Percy. Went out there farming after he'd finished with the Army. He's sure to be of the same frame of mind as I am. To cut a long tale short, I sold him the mineral rights when I was a bit—er—embarrassed. Had to sell the fellow something, and that seemed to be about all that was left."

Dan turned to say a word to Doris, but her attention was elsewhere. Head inclined, she was listening. Her eyes were directed to the orchard at the side of the barn, where the last of the apples hung heavy and conspicuous among the thinning leaves. There came the flat, whining creak of the orchard gate being opened. Hooves sounded on the hard-packed stone in the gateway from the road. Then, fifty yards away, slumped listlessly in the saddle, Grace Fairbrother appeared round the corner of the old tithe barn.

Lawson-Hope stepped forward. He made an impatient gesture in her direction.

"That's no way to sit a horse. Slovenly."

She straightened immediately. Gathering the reins, she wheeled the horse round and urged it out of sight again behind the barn. They heard the clatter of hooves at the gateway, heard the gate slam shut. Moments later they could watch her going at a flying gallop across the valley back towards her home.

"Extraordinary." The Squire shook his head. "Peculiar, like her father." To him, bad horsemanship was the eighth deadly sin. "Strange he should imagine we'd want a mine here." He waved goodbye to Dan and Doris, and turned for the village. "Keeps his hand in at that business stuff for when he gets back to London. Ah, well, no harm's done."

Doris's gaze lingered on the receding figure going across the valley. She imagined that Grace was fleeing from something repugnant to her. And Grace, Doris thought, was not without influence with her father. Lawson-Hope's tactless remark had been made at the worst possible time.

"I wouldn't be too sure of that," Doris Archer said quietly, in a tone of mild rebuke.

The numerous windows of Fairbrother's farm office —which had been converted from an old army hut— afforded a good view of nearly half the farm. It was possible for a farm manager working at his desk to keep an eye on most of what was going on outside, although the pastures and plough-fields down by the trout stream were hidden by a slight rise in the intervening land. The view from the office door took in more of the land and much of the squarely built farmhouse itself, separated from the yards and outbuildings by a broad gravel drive which swept round the house and a hundred yards down to the road.

The office was well sited—perhaps too well—for when he was tied to the desk trying to catch up with his paper work, Philip Archer often unconsciously looked through the windows and became absorbed in what the workmen were doing outside, either in the yard and sheds or in the fields.

"Must remember to keep my nose down close to the desk or we won't finish." He smiled up at the girl standing by his chair.

She was in her early twenties. There were freckles at the corners of her long-lashed tawny eyes and on the bridge of her nose.

When she spoke it was with a lively eagerness in keeping with her unruly auburn hair, but in repose her mouth was pensive, full, almost sensuous.

Her femininity was not masked by her rough breeches and jersey. The firm contour of her bosom and the long curve of her hips gave an unexpected womanliness to the simple, workmanlike clothes she wore.

"Stick a pin in me if I start slacking," Phil said.

Jane Maxwell nodded.

"Harpoon you to death if needs be," she said cheerfully.

She moved to the chair beside him and sat down. She watched him out of the corner of her eye and within seconds his attention strayed outside again.

Jane leant across and quietly took the pencil from his slack fingers. A strand of hair for a moment touched his cheek and he gave her a half-embarrassed, half-apologetic smile, but she could see his mind remained outside.

"Dream on," she said. He hadn't really noticed her. "I'll have to do it myself."

The pencil she took from him travelled lightly over columns of figures in an analysis of the farm's egg production for the month. Presently she sat back. The work had been done while Phil dreamed.

"Good for us. The new pullets that have come into lay are doing very well—they're more than earning their keep."

"So are you." He did not look round, but, chin in hand, gazed out of the window.

She realized he was barely conscious of her. She was but one strand in the complex pattern around him—the pattern of the good life as he knew it—and she could almost guess his thoughts. You worked on the land, he'd be thinking—twelve, fourteen hours a day, maybe, and in return you were satisfied. The best enrichment of the soil was the steady labour of man. Before him were the fields he and his people had brought to their present autumnal bounty. The essentials of life were before his eyes—wood, water, land and food. In his own hands were the strength and will to work the soil.

Cities and their gargantuan industrial needs meant nothing to him, she knew. Men could have the produce of the bountiful land, but if they touched the land itself, he for one would reach out for whatever weapons were at hand to defend it from their greed. The land was sacred and whoever touched it would be answerable to Phil Archer.

Jane stirred restlessly at his side.

"I often wonder if I'm keeping somebody out of a job who really needs the money," she said.

She was the daughter of an old-established county family, born a few miles outside Cheltenham in the lovely Elizabethan house where her family had lived for three hundred years. It was said that the family owed its initial prosperity to the charms of a girl who had smiled at Henry VIII, but the Maxwells had never been able to prove or to disprove the rumour.

Jane had been educated at boarding school. She could have chosen almost any life for herself. And here she was—a qualified poultry girl analysing egg production and getting worked up over ironstone.

"The mine's a pretty awful thought, isn't it?" she asked, but Phil seemed in no hurry to come out of his reverie.

If she was realistic about it, she reasoned, she would hand in her notice, pack up and go home, for the mining business was no affair of hers. There were other villages and other farms she could work on if she wanted to. But she could not help feeling sorry for people who were really affected by it—people like Phil.

"Jolly frustrating after the good work you've put in here, Phil. I'm sorry."

He turned and looked her full in the face, smiling at last.

She could not meet his eyes. In her heart she knew there was a stronger, more personal reason why she did not want to leave the farm, to go away from the trouble that loomed ahead—a reason that had to be smothered.

He turned away and looked out of the window again.

"Grace!" he snapped.

Jane started.

Phil was looking anxiously across the field.

"Grace, go easy!" He grasped Jane's arm. "Look at the way she's driving that horse—much too hard!"

They ran from the office and clambered over the stout fence that led from the yard into the pasture. The mare was galloping towards them, with Grace crouched well forward in the saddle.

"Don't charge at the gate!" Phil called. "You'll never turn the horse after that gallop!"

As she heard his voice, Grace drew on the reins.

Somehow she pulled up within a foot or two of the gate and Phil reached out for the bridle of the trembling horse. Grace slid to the ground and immediately the animal shied away.

"Been going it, haven't you, Grace?"

Phil's voice was quiet, controlled, but Jane noticed in it a quality of stern reproach. If he had spoken to her like that, she would have squirmed. Not so Grace. There was a cold, angry restlessness in her manner that seemed to brush aside Phil's remonstrance.

Self-possessed, Grace spared the horse a quick glance and flicked casually at her boot with her whip.

The horse turned. Phil's hand slipped down its sweaty flank and beneath its belly to the girth, which he loosened a little. Without another glance at Grace, he slowly walked the mare across the yard towards the stable, talking softly to her as he went.

Jane watched the other girl appraisingly. In her own impulsive way Jane had long ago decided what she wanted. She wanted to be useful and she wanted to live in the country—and just recently she found she wanted Phil. It hurt her to mask her feelings, but she did it for his sake. His employer's daughter was too possessive—and might well become a stubborn enemy.

"You did ride the mare rather hard," she said quietly, echoing Phil.

Grace whirled to stare at Jane, her eyes indignant and resentful, her face clouded with suspicion and suffering. Jane was suddenly conscious of a great rivalry welling up between them.

Guiltily she turned, hoping Grace had not noticed the hostility which must have been evident in her own eyes, and hurried back to the farm office.

III

"**N**o, you can't come in."

Chuckling, Phil Archer ignored Christine's protest and entered the bathroom. It had been converted from a bedroom big enough to hold a couple of four-posters.

His sister straightened up from the washbasin, a trickle of pink toothpaste running down over her chin.

"I said you can't come in. I haven't finished."

"I'm in."

Phil dragged his bath towel from the rail and flicked it in the direction of the stooping figure. Christine's yelp of indignation came at the same moment that she rinsed her mouth. Spluttering, she rounded on her brother.

"Won't you ever grow up?"

"Can't resist puppy-fat," he laughed. He was in his mid-twenties and often teased her with being a child, although the actual difference in their ages was very little. "When you blossom into womanhood and qualify to wear your brand-new clothes——"

"Oh, shut up."

Phil looked at his sister's round face and mop of fair hair. He contrasted her compact, neat figure with Grace Fairbrother's lean, bird-like elegance. The difference between town and country bred was marked—Grace with her carefully planned make-up and fashionable clothes, Christine with her natural colouring and a wardrobe showing she sacrificed much to the everyday demands of practicality.

The smile faded at the thought of Grace.

"What's the trouble?" Christine rubbed her face vigorously with the towel. "Still brooding about the ironstone?"

"Maybe."

He brushed past her and turned both taps in the basin full on.

"You and Grace haven't had a quarrel, have you?" The casualness in Christine's voice was part deliberate, part mocking. "It seems ages since you went out with her. I hear she charged in and out of here like a highwayman yesterday."

Phil rubbed the foaming soap energetically between his palms and started to lather his face. "It's difficult for me to be friendly with her when her father's creating such havoc."

"With the village—or with your job?" Again the faint edge of half-sympathetic mockery.

"Both."

There was a busy fluttering of startled house sparrows under the eaves. From outside came a great puffing of steam and grinding of iron-rimmed wheels. Brother and sister moved to the window to watch an ancient traction engine towing an unwieldy, dull red threshing box into the yard at Brookfield Farm.

"Dad's threshing out some oats today," Christine said. "Dear brother Jack and Walter Gabriel are both coming in to give a hand."

Phil glanced up at the sky before going back to the washbasin.

"Hope it keeps dry for 'em," he said. Lathering up again, he examined his own reflection in the mirror as Christine wrapped her dressing-gown more tightly around her and left the bathroom.

Phil sluiced water over his neck and ears, relishing his early morning wash. It never failed to amuse the rest of the family that he seemed to require so much energy and lather to get himself clean. He snorted, his mouth framed in soap and his eyes tight shut.

While he shaved Phil tried to plan his working day. As farm manager he had to keep busy five men, Jane Maxwell, the boy they got under the Y.M.C.A. scheme and Angus the cowman. His planning for the day depended to a large extent on the weather—and just lately it had come to depend a great deal on Fairbrother, too. Recently Fairbrother had steadfastly refused to approve any long-term plans for the farm, confident that they would have to be cancelled when opencast mining started.

Phil was puzzled by Fairbrother's certainty that the scheme would go through. He had thought around the problem until he was dizzy.

"Forget it," he told his reflection with a helpless shrug. "Life's too short."

Christine was already at breakfast with her father when Phil got downstairs. The glow of the range reflected back from the red-tiled floor, giving the large, old-fashioned kitchen, with its horse-brasses framing the mantelpiece, a familiar, welcoming warmth.

He sniffed appreciatively.

"Bacon and mushrooms."

Dan Archer grunted.

"Picked 'em last night when I was going round the fields with my gun. And I don't want any cracks from you about shooting them down."

Phil went to collect his plate from his mother, who was dishing the bacon hot from the pan. He remembered how, when he was a child, he used to cling to her as he dipped bread into the sizzling fat while she was frying, and how she had always given him the sharp warning, "Mind your *eyes*, Phil. If the fat jumps it'll blind you."

Now she said, "Don't bolt it or you'll get indigestion."

The phone rang before they had finished breakfast. Dan pushed back his chair noisily on the tiles and went to answer it. They could hear his voice in the hall and knew it was the Squire calling. Silence fell over them and when Dan came back the expression on his face was grave. He reached for his old trilby on the peg behind the door.

"The Squire says he's heard from his cousin Percy in Kenya. Seems Colonel Percy hasn't got the mineral rights to the estate. He let 'em go during the war to some chap called Crawford."

The back door was shut and Dan was gone almost before the others realised what he had said.

"But——That means——" Doris Archer stared blankly at her children.

"It means there's nobody here now to stop Fairbrother going ahead with his beastly mine whenever he likes. We'll all be dug up and sent packing," Christine said bitterly.

Phil sat for a moment, frowning, taking in the news. He banged his fist down on the table.

"Makes me feel like throwing my job in," he snapped, leaving the table abruptly.

Outside, in the yard, he was greeted with a throaty:

"'Ullo, Phil, me old pal, me old beauty."

He looked up to see a pair of rheumy old eyes, crinkled with a mixture of craftiness and benevolence, regarding him intently.

After a curt "Morning, Walter," Phil was grateful that the engine of his employer's shooting brake purred to life at the first touch of the starter. He was in no mood to talk with garrulous Walter Gabriel, who single-handed and without much success tried to run the forty-odd-acre farm next door to Brookfield.

"'Ow be things up at the rich man's table, then?" Walter asked maliciously.

He looked grubbier and untidier than anybody in the district. His wellingtons were patched with a pink, fleshy-looking bit of inner tube, his dungarees clumsily darned in two shades of washed-out blue. His striped, tieless shirt had no stud, but was held together at the collar by a safety-pin.

Without being provoked into an answer, Phil jerked his thumb in the direction of his father, striding through the yard towards the thresher. He let in the clutch and drove off, leaving Walter to stare quizzically at Dan's ancient farm worker, Simon, and Bill Slater, a pale, sickly-looking London lad who had recently come to work at Brookfield.

Simon spat reflectively into a puddle.

"Must 'ave got out o' bed wrong side, I reckon," he said, and led the way towards the thresher.

By the time Phil reached Fairbrother's some of his bad humour had dissipated. He swung the shooting brake up the drive and round the back of the house in the crisp, morning air. He had a pleasant thrill of admiration when he saw Jane Maxwell coming across the yard, body thrown forward at an angle and head well down, hauling a trolley loaded with wooden egg crates.

"That's too heavy for you, Jane. Ease up." He opened the gate wide and joined her.

"Morning, Phil. Collection day. I was taking them to the loading platform. This isn't so bad, but it was pretty heavy going through the mud from the hen batteries."

"Come on. I'll give you a hand." He felt the easy movement of the girl at his side and the additional impetus of the trolley as she tugged at it. He smiled. "All right, go easy. Don't run me down."

He watched her out of the corner of his eye, warmed by the thought that she was pulling her weight. She always did, he reflected. It seemed odd that such a finely-made cultured creature as Jane should apparently get so much enjoyment out of trying to turn herself into a dray horse, tugging at a load far too heavy for her. With something of a shock he realised that he was enjoying it too. There was a friendliness, a sense of comradeship in their progress across the slippery yard which he well knew would not have been there if any of the other farm hands were hauling the load with him.

She looked up and to avoid her eyes he glanced through the open doors of the garage, adjacent to the farm sheds. Beside Fairbrother's solid-looking, black saloon and Grace's more flashy sports car was a large car he had never seen before.

"Posh car," he observed.

"Oh, great goings on last night, according to the maid when she came to collect the eggs for the house," Jane panted. "Important guest from Felpersham. Or London, or both, or something. Much fuss over the dinner being just so. More fuss over whether the wines were going to be right. All hands on deck to make a favourable impression because it's the first time they've met him. A really special effort."

"Probably Fairbrother's income-tax bloke," Phil grinned, bringing the trolley to a halt by the covered loading platform at the edge of the drive. "Anyhow, whoever he is I wouldn't say no to his car."

"His name's Crawford."

"What!" Phil almost dropped a crate of eggs. "Jane—are you sure?" He looked at her intently.

"That's what the maid said."

Phil swore.

"Why, Phil—what's the matter?"

"Tell you later. Can't stop to explain now. I've got to make a phone call."

He went briskly to the farm office and rang up Brookfield. He was halfway through telling his mother what he had discovered before he even thought of asking himself whether he was being disloyal to his employer. But by then Doris was plying him with questions he felt bound to answer.

"All right, Phil." His mother's voice came from the other end. "I'll tell your father straight away and if he thinks he ought to he can ring the Squire and tell him. Are you quite sure it's the man who has the mining rights?"

"Wait a sec, Mum."

At the sound of voices outside Phil put the phone down and went to the office door. A smartly dressed, middle-aged man was behind the wheel of the big car in the garage, chatting to Grace, while Fairbrother deposited his travelling case and briefcase on the back seat.

The car purred smoothly out of the garage and the man was getting out for final handshakes when Phil went back to the phone. "Crawford's just off, Mum. I don't know whether it's too late to do anything or not, but you'd better tell Dad—quick."

He replaced the receiver and moved to the door again, anxious to get a closer look at the man who held the fate of the farming land of Ambridge in his hands, but Crawford's car was already accelerating down the drive. Hands behind his back, Fairbrother walked to the corner of the house to watch the car until it disappeared out of sight on the road.

Grace gave a final wave, turned and saw Phil. She half turned away, then changed her mind and came across the yard towards him, smiling shyly, a little anxiously.

Grimly Phil noticed she was wearing a smart town suit in place of her customary country tweeds. The atmosphere seemed to tighten and, worried by a feeling of something impending, he wanted to turn away and shut the door against her. But mere politeness held him there until she came up.

He tried to speak civilly, but a bitter edge was on his voice.

"Kept it to yourself pretty well, didn't you?"

The appeal in her dark eyes told him she knew what he was talking about.

"You must have had quite a laugh," he went on, "during the past few days, knowing Crawford had the mineral rights." He was aware of the injustice of venting his bitterness on the girl. It was her father who was to blame, but he wanted to hurt her, to allay his own disquiet. "I hope you realise what you're doing with your secrecy."

"Phil, I'm not so keen on this ironstone business as you think."

There was apology and a pathetic anxiousness not to make more trouble in the way she spoke. Phil reined in his bitterness and when he spoke again it was more calmly.

"Then you've got a darn funny way of showing it. You could have dropped a word to me about Crawford, couldn't you? Don't try to tell me you didn't know about him ages ago."

"I couldn't say anything because he was out of the country until yesterday. But I admit I knew about him."

"And took damn good care nobody else found out," he snapped.

Her cheeks flushed and her eyes glittered dangerously. Her head came up high in defiance, but when she spoke her voice was quiet.

"One of the things I learnt when I was young was 'honour thy father and thy mother'. If my father tells me something in confidence I respect his wishes. I may not agree with everything he does but that doesn't alter the fact that I have a duty to him. Nobody can make me disloyal to him—not even you, Phil. I won't break his confidences even if they mean the end of—of other attachments."

She turned and went quickly away. He was in half a mind to follow, but Fairbrother called from the corner of the house and beckoned him over.

"Philip, what's the telephone number of that printer chap in Hollerton?" With Crawford's car out of sight Fairbrother turned briskly to business. "I want some notices printed. I've decided to call a public meeting in the village hall."

"A meeting? What for, sir?" Phil frowned.

Fairbrother rubbed his hands.

"I'm going to explain to anybody who's interested just what the ironstone scheme's going to mean to Ambridge!" he announced.

During the next few days while the printing order went through, Fairbrother spent much of his time in the village, in case anyone wished to talk to him. He spent what he considered wasted hours in the Bull, drinking pint after pint of ale, but none of the men would let him buy them a drink and nobody bought him one. He stood at the bar window, pensive, alone, ignored for many hours and with plenty of time for reflection.

Ruefully he told himself he knew every inch of the view from the window of the public bar. From what he could see of Ambridge there was nothing exceptional about the place to cause anyone to kick up a fuss.

The main street was inclined to wander. The villagers seemed to consider that as it was wide enough for a horse there was no reason why five-ton lorries should not, in time, become used to it.

No one would gather from the straight line on the map that the street twisted as it bore sharply to the right to call in at the church with its adjoining vicarage, then veered to the left to incorporate the post office. From the post office to the Bull Inn the street pursued a fairly straight course. Small cottages with front gardens full of colourful, scented flowers and herbs lined this short stretch. The cottages had been built after the road itself became a road, as distinct from a well-travelled country lane. They had been built a long time after the Bull Inn was constructed, too, but intelligent forethought on the part of the Lawson-Hope family, squires of the village for many generations, had ensured that they were in keeping with the village scene.

Down at the bottom end, past the church, was the village school—much too elaborately constructed on the outside (according to the older people, who remembered the days when all classes were taught in one room) and with rather sketchy teaching inside (according, again, to those with long memories, who could recall the days when Miss Peterson, single-handed, had dinned the three R's and numerous other practical matters into the thick heads of her charges). Nowadays, some said, Miss Elsie Catcher only succeeded in teaching the children to model in clay, cut up the newspapers and be rude to their elders before they took the first available jobs in Borchester.

Behind the school was Blossom Hill, a local landmark which was a cloud of flowers in the spring, and a temptation to the schoolchildren from the moment the first green apples grew to the size of plums.

Fairbrother turned up the street, shielding his eyes from the glint of the sun on the two glasshouses forming the backbone of Jack Archer's smallholding, standing back from the point where the road split in two to form an island of carefully tended turf. This was the Ambridge village green with its smartly white-washed pavilion and the sight-screens contrasting with the green patch of turf which was Ambridge's particular pride, chained off and unmown now for the winter. The huge elms and the chestnut trees, which gave welcome shade to the cricket enthusiasts, were now almost bare of leaves.

At the other end of the green was Mattie Troach's smithy, still in part-time use, though a petrol pump had been built outside it as a gesture of competition with old Wainwright, who had a garage farther down the road.

Fairbrother walked moodily up the street towards his own farm, past the road that branched off to Brookfield and the Manor and on over the stone bridge spanning the River Am, the bridge which marks the far end of the village and which gives Ambridge its name. The Am was more of a stream than a river, but it held some of the finest trout south of the Scottish border.

To a certain extent Ambridge had moulded its people to its own pattern—slow, serene, old-fashioned, but dignified and wholesome. Fairbrother had spent many hours walking up and down the High Street and had failed to see why the villagers were so devoted to it, although he had to admit that the trout were good.

A paper flapping in the October breeze caught his eye. He paused for a moment to examine one of the two billboards in the village, smoothed the corner of the notice about his village meeting and tried to stop the wind tearing it. Here, outside the school, the church, the Bull and the village hall where the meeting was to be held, was posted his challenge to Ambridge.

"They won't like their medicine," he said softly. "But I wager they'll have to take it."

IV

O N THE night of the meeting Phil Archer walked
slowly from his home, hands deep within his
pockets and his shoulders hunched. It was a
cold, dank evening, though it was not the cold so much
as dejection which made him walk slowly.

The longer he put off going to the meeting, the
longer, he felt, Ambridge was his. He was conscious
of covert glances from the villagers he met on his way
to the village hall. As he had grown from a somewhat
turbulent boyhood, he had become more and more
like his father, who was sensible, reliable and a stranger
to panic. As long as Dan and his younger son looked
contented, the villagers felt that there would be some
kind of satisfactory solution to their problems.

But tonight Phil Archer walked alone. Dan Archer
stood silent and thoughtful in the middle of a group
of older man.

Short of a miracle which would show Fairbrother
that the village was a united community, as a mining
town could never be, there seemed no way of pre-
senting Ambridge's point of view.

By common accord, the women had stayed away
from the meeting. Instinctively, they expected trouble;
at best, strong language, at worst, broken heads.

Outside the hall, the village policeman leaned on
his bicycle.

"Evening," said Phil. "Expecting trouble, George?"

Inside, the chilly hall was not made much warmer
by a sulphurous smell coming from the choked-up

stove in the centre. The crowd drifted in, in twos and threes. There was an ominous silence which presaged trouble. Phil selected a seat inconspicuously at one side, anxious to avoid being called upon by either the villagers or Fairbrother to take sides. Days ago, he had decided that his loyalties were with the village and not with his employer, but he shrank from making public such an irrevocable decision and even at this stage hoped it might never be necessary.

Promptly at eight Fairbrother came in and walked slowly up the centre towards the stage. The subdued hum of conversation ceased. Phil was startled to see Grace, the only woman in the hall, walking firmly by her father's side.

He felt his heart reach out to her. She had come, he knew, so that she might stand between her father and violence. Any damage to her own sensitive spirit she would consider a fitting sacrifice of loyalty and love.

Sensing the bitter mood of the audience, Phil called "Grace!" as she passed. He wanted her to sit down in the hall with him, where at least she would be spared the worst of the storm of abuse which would certainly be directed towards the platform.

She heard him, because she flushed, but without looking at him she continued to the platform with her father.

Fairbrother began reasonably enough, explaining gently, with a persuasive voice, what increased prosperity would mean to the village. More trade for the Bull and the stores, better roads and other amenities because of increased revenue from the rates. He spoke of a better bus service, more houses, more electric light, and better cricket and soccer teams.

"Let's put Ambridge on the map," he said. "We want a railway station, a decent-sized store, garages, more motor cars. None of us will get rich out of food. Try to see this in a broader view, outside parochial boundaries. We live in a great little country. We haven't become great just by tilling the soil. We were a forgotten little barbarian outpost of Europe, before iron and steel and wool and cotton mills brought us power and greatness."

"Who wants power?" someone interrupted, in a voice scarcely above a whisper. "All we want is to be left alone to lead our own lives."

Ignoring him, Fairbrother went on elaborating his theme, a little academically, but with enough eloquence to convince Phil and Dan at least that from his point of view there was no alternative to mining the iron: it would be unpatriotic and uneconomic to leave it in the soil.

The meeting in general was in no mood to listen. Chairs creaked and boots scraped on the wooden floor. The villagers became increasingly restive, as he became increasingly forthright.

A fresh interruption came from a farmer in the well of the hall.

" What about loss of food production, eh? What've you got to say about that? Who is going to feed the miners? "

Fairbrother paused in the middle of a sentence, but before he could reply there was a buzz of comment from the hall.

"What about compensation?"

"Why can't you leave us alone?"

"Money-grubbing!"

"Go back to London."

"Clear off and leave us alone."

Helpless before the growing barrage, Fairbrother held up his hands in a vain appeal for silence. A flush spread up from his neck to his hair.

Phil noticed a subtle change in his bearing that revealed something of the grit and strength of character that had brought him to the top after an indifferent start in life.

"He owes his success to nobody but himself," Phil thought grudgingly. "But by golly, the man's a fighter."

He glanced across at Grace. She was staring straight ahead, not daring to look at her father or anyone else, striving to keep her emotions under control.

The noise in the hall subsided a little and Fairbrother took full advantage of it.

"I had hoped that at this meeting tonight we could fairly and without rancour try to see each other's point of view——"

"What about Crawford?" a voice called at Phil's elbow.

Phil saw Grace look sharply and angrily in his direction. He groaned inwardly, realising she attributed the question to him. Every move was now subject to suspicion, every word the breeding-place of misunderstanding. It was hopeless to think they would ever get back to their old footing.

Another more urgent voice made itself heard above the growlings of the meeting. Young Bill Slater was elbowing his way along the aisle up to the platform. Tousled and breathless, he waved urgently to Fairbrother and his strident Cockney voice rang out clearly.

"Mr. Fairbrother! Mr. Fairbrother! Better come quick! There's a fire up at your place!"

Bill Slater, a thin, small, undernourished product of outer London, was very rarely the centre of attention. He relished his moment in the limelight, even though he brought bad tidings. Every face in the meeting was turned his way, and every brain was trying to assess the significance of his statement.

From the platform, Fairbrother looked down incredulously at Slater. The youth had a reputation as a glib and convincing liar and Fairbrother's expression hardened at the sight of the pasty, defiant face staring up at him.

"If this is your idea of a joke——" he started severely.

"It's no joke! Go and look for yourself."

Bill spoke with a surly conviction which was just short of impudence. His round shoulders were hunched forward under his old raincoat, and his legs were planted wide across the aisle between the rows of chairs.

Dan and Phil Archer were already at the door of the village hall. An angry glow in the sky proclaimed that Bill Slater told the truth. Dan bellowed back into the hall.

"Come on, lads! It's a fire all right." He signalled to the man on the platform. "We'll do what we can, Mr. Fairbrother. Bill—you'd better go to the call-box and fetch the fire brigade. The rest of you come with me—it'll be twenty minutes before the brigade gets here!"

The meeting broke up. Half a dozen packed cars sped through the village and up the hill to Fairbrother's farm. In the back of Dan's car, Walter Gabriel puffed between Phil and his brother Jack.

"Got no love for Fairbrother," he wheezed in his

harsh voice. "But ironstone or no ironstone, we can't stand by and watch the place burn down."

"It's the ricks!"

Phil leaned forward anxiously, staring ahead as the car swept up the gravel drive to Fairbrother's farm. The ricks were close to the sheds and the garage. Once they were alight it would be hard to save the house.

"Jack—there's a water bowser and tractor over by the grain pits. Fetch it!" he snapped. "Walter—there's a hose in the garage!"

He was out of the car before it stopped. One rick was already well alight. It burnt so fiercely there was no hope of saving it. The showers of sparks it sent up landed on a couple of ricks close by and fired the thatches.

More cars slithered to a halt in the gravel drive and the occupants piled out. Men who, brief minutes before, had been hurling imprecations at Fairbrother during the meeting, grabbed sacks, tarpaulins, rakes, buckets—anything they could lay hands on from the yard and sheds—and unhesitatingly joined in fighting the blaze. They were farming folk who knew the serious consequences of losing a rick.

"Get the ladders from the barn! I'm going up on top to try and dowse the thatches."

"No, Phil, I'll go," Dan said. "You stay below. You're needed down here. You know the place."

On top of one of the ricks, flaying at the thatch with a sack, yanking out great tufts of smouldering straw and tossing them below, Dan caught occasional fleeting impressions of the general scene illuminated in the orange glow of the blazing rick.

Grace and Fairbrother driving up . . . Phil quick and cool, directing, informing, improvising . . . Walter and Jack fetching down great lumps of blazing hay with smoking, wooden rakes . . . Jane Maxwell lugging heavy buckets of water in each hand, her skirt already sodden from the sloppings of previous trips. . . .

Grace turned into the house and put on large kettles for tea. Swiftly she laid out biscuits and cake, before she stopped to think that she was taking it for granted that Phil and the men with him would succeed in saving the sheds, the garage and the house.

Someone had turned off the electricity and she had to work by the light which came from the gas jets under the kettle, and the ghoulish rise and fall of the flames against the dark sky.

She did not have time to feel afraid—time only to work out how many men would need the tea, and time to think that her dying love for Phil had leapt into new life, just as the ricks had burst into flame. She could hear his voice, loud, calm and firm, making full use of his knowledge of the farm, directing the volunteers who fought the blaze. There was something primitive and wholly satisfying in the fact that the man she loved was battling against one of the elements on her behalf.

A familiar throaty voice made itself heard in the confusion. "Dan! Dan, me old beauty!" Walter was halfway up the ladder. "Off this rick smartish! It's gettin' a hold! You'll be trapped!"

Dan took one look, realised the fire was gaining the upper hand and made for the ladder.

Nobody heard the fire-engine bell from the village with greater relief than Fairbrother, who was standing helplessly at the yard gate. He was rooted to the spot by cold indignation amounting almost to the kind of steely anger which is a motivating force in cold-blooded murder.

His narrowed eyes looked round at his neighbours—at Dan Archer, his legs firm on the lowest rung of the ladder; at Walter, moving as quickly and efficiently as a young man; at Phil, his young farm manager, hurriedly directing a knot of men to work; at Bill Slater, his quick hands tearing at smouldering hay and taking it well away from the sheds.

Slater. Fairbrother wondered why the youth angered him. He could not have known when he first saw him in Ambridge what an important part Bill was to play in his life. He was a nephew of Mrs. Perkins, Fairbrother vaguely recalled, who used to work in a factory on tractors or something, somewhere on the Thames bank. A chest ailment made it necessary for Bill to get more fresh air, and Dan Archer had taken him on as a gesture to Mrs. Perkins.

Fairbrother disliked Bill Slater instinctively; when he had discovered him teaching the young Y.M.C.A. lad employed on the farm to gamble at cards he had taken every advantage of the opportunity of giving Slater the rough edge of his tongue.

Slater had had another slanging over damaging the tractor, too. But such was the queer twist of fate that it was due to the insolent young puppy running the tractor over a rock outcrop and almost wrecking it that the ironstone was found.

Watching the rick blaze, Fairbrother tried to remember how long ago it was that they first discovered the ironstone under the farm. It seemed a long time. He thought of his dead wife and how he had moved out to the farm, to a fresh environment, to make the bereavement easier for Grace. And he remembered their studious efforts to become a part of village life.

His jaw hardened. It stood to reason the ironstone had to be dug out, however much these farming folk protested. Their outburst at the meeting, their mulish obstinacy and resistance to change, had hurt him so much that in this moment he hated them all and would willingly have seen England one huge industrial city from Northumberland to Penzance. . . .

One of the firemen was beckoning to him, and Fairbrother hurried to see what he wanted, grateful for something to do.

The fire brigade took over and the volunteers stood watching until, some minutes later, the fire was out. One rick was a total loss and part of another ruined, and the knot of men standing around thought of all the stock the burnt hay would have fed when grazing was short.

"Reckon Phil'll be missing that around about next March, Walter," Dan grunted. "Bad luck."

"Ay." Walter's aged, crafty-kind features brightened. "Put an end to the meetin' and Fairbrother's ironstone natterin', though, didn't it?"

"I don't think so."

They turned at the sound of Fairbrother's voice. His face was gaunt in the beams of car headlights switched on to illumine the scene after the fire was put out.

"The fire wasn't an accident." He waited for the words to sink in. "One of the men from the brigade found a paraffin drum in the hedge."

Fairbrother squared his shoulders and Dan glimpsed the same rugged determination and strength of will that showed through his veneer for a moment when he was on the stage of the village hall facing the jeers of the audience.

"A demonstration of Ambridge's dislike for me, Mr. Archer. Sabotage!" The sibilance he gave the word made it doubly emphatic. "All right! If that's the game Ambridge wants to play, it's a fight from now on—and be damned to 'em."

The little group of men, sweating, pleased that their work had almost eliminated the need for the fire brigade, took the tea Grace offered them in amazed silence. The big man from the city did not seem to realise what the loss of a rick meant to a country-man. Any farming man would travel a dozen miles to help a neighbour in a fire such as this. Some thanks were due.

Instead, Fairbrother repeated "Be damned to 'em."

V

I N THE next few days a number of other things happened—things which Fairbrother called, bitterly, "belligerent incidents".

A gate was lifted off and some of Fairbrother's pedigree herd of Ayrshires strayed down the road past the Archers' farm, down the village street to the green, where they were promptly rounded up by the policeman and impounded.

Another time it was his sheep that were allowed to escape. Late-night revellers returning home from a dance in Felpersham ran into the flock on a bend of the road. A couple of ewes were injured and had to be destroyed.

On another occasion Fairbrother's cowman arrived one morning to find the milking machines and dairy smeared with thick engine oil. After that Fairbrother ordered padlocks on all the outbuildings.

The atmosphere was electric. The whole village was under a pall of suspicion and gloom. Neighbour eyed neighbour speculatively and private thoughts as to who could be responsible for the outrages tainted the pleasure of normal social intercourse. Even in the bar at the Bull, the one place where the grossest insults could be hurled in the broad, earthy humour of the countryside without offence being taken, the men of Ambridge were cautious. Darts, crib and dominoes, where before a constant stream of ribbing and back-chat usually provided half the enjoyment in the games, now took place to an accompaniment of monosyllabic grunts and whispered comments.

Brookfield Farm did not escape from the increasing tension.

"It won't do," Dan said in exasperation one morning at breakfast. "It just won't do. Things are bad enough as it is without all this tomfoolery and it certainly doesn't do our case a bit of good. It's enough to make Fairbrother dig his toes in and not give an inch. That's what I'd do if it was me, anyway."

"So would anybody." Phil viciously speared his last sausage with his fork. "I wish I knew who was doing it. I'd knock hell out of 'em."

His mother looked shocked.

"So I would," he said doggedly. "If only the fools realised it's not Fairbrother they're hurting—it's me! I've got to carry the can for what happens on the farm. Look to that rick fire. Who suffers? The stock, because it's their fodder—and me, because it's my responsibility to feed 'em. If they want to get at Fairbrother let 'em go and burn his blasted plastics factory down in London or his factory in Felpersham."

In bad-tempered haste he finished his breakfast, grabbed his jacket and flung out of the house.

"He's quite right, of course," Christine said quietly. "They're taking it out on Phil and the stock."

"I can't help feeling sorry for Grace," Doris said. "It must be a very nasty feeling for her. It's a shocking way to treat Grace and her father."

"They brought it on themselves."

Dan was surprised at Christine's dispassionate summing up, although it reflected the attitude of the village in general.

"That shows you what things have come to," he

said to Doris after his daughter had left for her work at Borchester milk depôt. "Chris and Grace used to be thick as thieves. She'd never have said that a month or two ago."

"Phil and Grace seem at loggerheads, too," Doris said. "He hardly ever talks about her now—and when he does he gets moody and upset."

Phil had his reasons for being put out. He knew from Fairbrother's curtness and from Grace's excuses to keep away from him, that he, of all people, was suspected of firing the ricks. Couldn't they see that he would never wantonly strike at the land, which could not strike back?

He pretended, mulishly, that he had noticed nothing. A pretence of stupidity was now his greatest defence, but he was thinking hard, trying to see their point of view. It may be, he admitted to himself grudgingly, that a farm manager in his position would resort to violence in order to frighten intruders away from the beloved farm. A man might do damage in order that a greater good would come of it.

Well, let them suspect him. He didn't care. And Grace could go to blazes if she was fool enough to take her father's part. Meanwhile, he would keep his own counsel, and not even confide in his mother and father.

For the next day or two Dan was busy around the farm. Two more fine calves were born. Some of his pigs had to be got away to the bacon factory and, as the last of the leaves began to fall, a dozen acres were ploughed and harrowed ready for drilling winter wheat and beans. One day he had occasion to go up to Fairbrother's to see Phil. He found only Jane Maxwell in the office. They chatted in desultory fashion for a while, but fairly soon the conversation turned to farming topics. Soon they were in a deep discussion and for the first time Dan really got to know her. It did not take him long to realise that this knowledgeable, pretty young lady with the unruly auburn hair and freckles had an instinctive sort of communion with the countryside.

"By George," he said finally, "you're one of us, Jane!"

"What a nice thing to say!" She smiled and glanced out of the window. "Phil's here."

It may have been only his fancy, but he thought she took care to avoid his eyes. He turned to the office door.

Phil came striding across the gravel, head thrust forward, jaw set, his face a mask of smouldering anger. He banged into the office and gave the door a rough kick that slammed it behind him.

"I'm packing in," he snapped.

"You're what?" asked Dan incredulously.

"I'm chucking it up—resigning!"

"Why?"

Phil calmed a little at the flat, matter-of-fact tone of his father.

"Know what Fairbrother just said when I went to ask him about one or two things on the farm? Said he was too busy with ironstone to have his mind cluttered up——" Phil snorted. "—his own words —*cluttered up* with farming. From now on it's all my pigeon."

He slumped down in a chair and glared out of the window.

"Look out there."

Dan and the girl joined him and he made a sweeping gesture with his hand.

"The mine'll tear a hole right across the farm like the Grand Canyon. There'll be a bit of land this side and a bit on the other—and I'm supposed to run it as a farm. It's hopeless! Crazy!"

He got up and paced around disgustedly.

Dan, thinking about the reorganisation involved, could well understand Phil's concern. He would be hopelessly overstocked, the rotation of his crops would be disorganised, labour and time wasted in getting from one part of the farm to the other would be incalculable. And when the mining was over and the muddled soil put back, the traditional character of the land would be lost.

Farmers of Dan's generation knew their fields like friends. Each had its character and its capabilities. What thrived on one was a failure on another. Each had to be known and treated accordingly. Phil would be farming an unknown quantity. . . .

"You're not serious about resigning, are you, Phil?" The soft warmth of Jane's voice interrupted Dan's thoughts.

"I am, you know. The atmosphere's pretty sticky nowadays. It's no fun to work here." He turned his back on them and after a few moments went on sombrely, "Besides, I don't want the worry. I don't think I'm capable of keeping the place going. I'm dead scared. I haven't got the confidence or experience to cope."

There was a short silence, then:

"Don't throw up everything you've achieved, Phil. You can do it. I know you can."

Jane was standing at his shoulder.

"Don't go away from here. It looks pretty black but it can be done. We'll find it's not so bad when we get down to it."

Dan saw the kindling interest and gratitude in his son's eyes.

"I wonder," he said to himself, and then, aloud, "Of course, I'll help too, if you think I can."

The pair started as though they had temporarily forgotten he was there.

"Oh—will you, Dad? Thanks." Phil's voice was calm and steady. His anger had gone.

"You won't resign, Phil?" Jane asked.

"Well—not yet."

After supper that evening father and son found themselves talking about Jane.

"Nice girl, Jane." Dan eyed his son shrewdly. "Make a darn good wife for some young farmer."

"That's a fact! She understands. You don't have to waste time explaining things."

Dan was still pondering over Phil's unvarnished enthusiasm long after his son had gone to bed. He locked up for the night and when he returned to the fireside Doris' quizzical eyes were on him.

"Penny for 'em," she said.

"I was just thinking, love—it's difficult not to make comparisons between Jane and Grace, isn't it?"

"Yes, but they're such very different people, Dan."

Doris folded her hands over the knitting in her lap and considered.

Her plump face was grave as she looked into the fire, seeing there pictures which were not for Dan to share. A son's wife was so important to a woman that not even someone as understanding as Dan could possibly trace her thoughts.

Jane, she knew, would perhaps be perfect from Phil's point of view. She would always be rooted to the land, she had made her choice and would stick to it. Jane worked hard, enjoyed life, never intruded her personality too much. She was pretty, vivacious, and presumably good company.

But there was something else. Doris groped for the idea which was troubling her. Perhaps it was all that red hair, that full mouth, that gave her the impression that love for Jane might well drag a man down into a whirlpool of sensuousness from which it would be difficult to escape. A doting husband was laughable anywhere, but in the country, he was pitiable. Jane loved laughter and company, but everything about her seemed to Doris' prejudiced eyes to be on the surface. About Grace there was something cool and remote, something ennobling that would lift the man she loved up with her into a higher plane, where spiritual values transmuted everyday life, so that love would be always fresh and untarnished.

"I'm very sorry for Grace," Doris said presently. "It's the ironstone that's come between her and Phil, Dan—a sort of iron curtain. That wasn't her doing. It was Fairbrother's. Still, there it is. She's on one side, Phil's on the other."

"And Jane happens to be on the same side as our Phil, eh?"

She looked up, troubled.

"Well, whatever side you're on, I s'pose you're right, love." Dan got up, yawned and went upstairs to bed.

He saw Grace the following day. He was on his way up to the Manor with his gun and Lass, the dog, to join other tenant farmers who had been invited by the Squire for a day's shooting, when Grace passed him on the road in her sports car and pulled up a few yards farther on.

"Can I give you a lift, Mr. Archer?"

"Ay, thank you, Grace, if you don't mind the dog's dirty feet. I'm on my way up to the Manor."

He put his gun in the back of the car and settled Lass between his knees. There was an awkward silence until he said:

"We don't see much of you these days, Grace."

"I didn't think you'd want to." She spoke sharply. "I thought we'd been shown pretty definitely what Ambridge thinks about us."

"Don't blame the sabotage on all Ambridge," Dan said. "We don't like it any more than you do. Most likely it's just a bunch of young hotheads who are always spoiling to do a bit of damage. Now they've got an excuse."

"D'you think that's really what it is?" She seemed pathetically anxious for reassurance.

The car pulled up at the Manor gates and Dan got out with a friendly smile.

"In any case, the quarrel isn't with you, love, is it?"

"No, it's——" She slammed home the gear and the car bounded forward.

Dan ruminated as he walked up the drive to the Manor that maybe the only hope Ambridge had of diverting Fairbrother from his ironstone scheme was through his daughter. But, he reflected, she had been made to suffer enough without any help from them.

He was the last to arrive at the gunroom where the others had assembled ready for the day's sport. He did not hear the expected talk of guns and shooting and how to train gun dogs. Nor was there the customary taking of bets or arranging sweepstakes on the day's bag.

The topic was ironstone. Impossible to get away from the darned stuff, these days, Dan mused.

One farmer was saying, "Trouble is we don't know what happened between Fairbrother and this fellow Crawford."

Another grunted, "Can't expect me to put money back into my place if they're going to tear it to bits next week, can you?"

"Makes you feel like chucking up," voiced a third.

The Squire came in and stood for a while listening. Then the men became conscious he was there and the talk died down.

"Believe me, my sympathies are with you," Lawson-Hope said. "I only wish I had some definite news myself."

"Why don't you see Fairbrother, sir?" a farmer rapped out suddenly. "If anybody's entitled to know what's going on, you are."

"I doubt whether I'd hold my temper if I saw him alone," Lawson-Hope replied, after considering for a moment. "But I'll visit him on your behalf if one of you will come with me."

Silence fell on the group. Then a voice from the back said clearly and emphatically, "Dan Archer."

"Ay, he can keep his temper better than any of us here."

There was a faint murmur of laughter among the group.

Lawson-Hope sought out Dan from the other farmers.

"What about it, Mr. Archer?"

It was a decision Dan wished he could avoid. What

right had he to stick his nose in? What about Phil? Would he embarrass him in his job with Fairbrother? What about Grace, cold-shouldered by everybody, including Phil?

But there was also Ambridge. . . . He knew the answer that was expected of him.

"All right, sir," Dan said quietly. "I'll come with you."

Studying the sober faces of the farmers as they filed from the gunroom, Tom Forrest, the Squire's game-keeper, reflected that they were a glum-looking lot. He was filled with a new sense of responsibility. Squire would look to him to brighten an otherwise unhappy day by providing them with some good shooting.

"Got some good sport lined up for us, Tom, you old faggot?" Walter Gabriel fell into step beside him and Tom, a cautious man through long associa-tion with sporting guns, saw with relief that the muzzles of Walter's ancient piece were pointing to the sky. There was a yellowy glint on one of the hammers where it had been broken and brazed, the stock was split in a couple of places and the small of the butt was bound with strong if grubby blind cord.

"Don't matter what I puts up, I doubt if you'll hit any on't with that thing, Walter."

"Give you a tanner every time I misses if you give me a tanner every time I hits," Walter said stoutly and marched off to exchange a few insults with another of his friends.

The day did not start off too well. There did not seem to be much about. Squire had been walking up the partridge since the first of September and the birds, growing wary and wild, were out of one end of a field faster than the guns could come in the other.

Bound to be a bit slow, Tom told himself, with the first flush of partridge shooting gone and not enough leaves down yet to justify driving the coverts for pheasant. Subconsciously he prayed that it would turn out to be a good day's shooting. It might be the last. He could not see the game hanging around if the place was torn apart by mining schemes.

"What about it, Tom?" The voice of the man who had married his sister when she was housekeeping up at the Manor cut across his thoughts.

"I reckon it'll be all right, Dan. We've got them rabbits to walk up that I stunk out a couple of nights ago and I reckoned on driving the stream and that bit of marsh for duck and the odd snipe or pheasant." He bent down and ran expert hands over Dan's dog, Lass. "There'll be plenty for her to do. We'll drive for a few partridges and hare this afternoon, then we can work the hedges for rabbits and any pheasants that are lying out."

At the end of the first hour they had bagged a few rabbits that bolted from tussocks where they were lying. The only incident that raised a smile among the men was a wild shot of Walter's that rattled a galvanised iron trough a good yard above where a rabbit moved.

The wind got up a bit, bringing with it a fine and penetrating rain just as they were going to walk a kale patch where Tom thought they might put up a pheasant or two. At a nod from the Squire he waved the guns through.

"There's stoppers on the other end. They'll get up all right."

But the pheasant ran and refused to fly and a small covey of French partridge followed their example. The farmers, stepping over the kite-tail stoppers Tom had earlier placed there, emerged from the other side of the kale wet through to the waist. From this point it was possible to see right across the valley to Fairbrother's land, where the mineralogist's drill rig stood out gaunt against the skyline, seeming to cast a shadow right over them.

"Not much doing so far, Tom."

There was a hint of irritation in the Squire's voice—an irritation that Tom knew was felt by all the men, not directed at *him* for failing so far to provide them with much sport, but directed against what the drill symbolised. Tom saw it in small ways: Joe Blower cuffing his dog when it failed to come immediately to heel, although it had been working well; Squire himself, peppering a rabbit that was an easy shot, not bothering to take it with his second barrel, but leaving it to someone else; Dan, usually meticulous, failing to thumb back his safety catch when he clambered over a gate; another farmer pulling off at a towerer when the partridge was already dead and falling.

"There's plenty about all right, sir," Tom told the Squire. "It'll come."

He led the way across a slimy green plank spanning a deep ditch, scattering grain from the bag on his back among the roots on the other side. Pheasants wandered miles in search of acorns unless they were encouraged to remain on his own beat. The thought gave rise to another—one of the lads of the village had recently acquired a lurcher. The nose of a bull terrier and the speed of a greyhound would very soon reduce his hare population, Tom considered. Not

66

that he had ever caught the lad, but it wouldn't do any harm to let him know he had his eye on him.

There was a sound of rending wood and a sudden yelp behind him. He turned in time to see Walter Gabriel plunging waist deep into the muddy ditch from the broken plank. His gun, broken at the breech, waved wildly in his hand as he fought for his balance and the pink cylinders of two cartridges leapt from it, spun in the air and fell with a plop into the water.

It seemed to be the turning point of the day. The gloom dissipated in the broad grins and leg-pulling of the men watching Walter drag himself, cursing, from the ditch. His trousers clung round his wiry legs and fine jets of water spurted from the eyelet holes of his boots. He squelched around making much fuss in abortive attempts to dry himself and when at last he announced he was ready to carry on, he discovered that somehow, in struggling out of the ditch, he had plugged the muzzles of his gun with mud.

From the moment they got on the move again everything went well. Tom took Dan with him, worked his way round the roots and started to drive. They put up fourteen brace of partridge that went away very fast. Six brace fell to the guns, even Walter managing to take one fore and aft. "A bob, that'll cost me," Tom said. Down in the water meadows there were hare and more rabbits, mallard and a few teal. There was another sharp storm, but by now the men were warmed to their task and when they broke for sandwiches, beer and coffee Tom was gratified when the Squire said, "B'jove, Tom, didn't realise we had quite so much stuff about."

Lawson-Hope beckoned Dan Archer over to the

tailboard of the shooting brake and slipped the cap off a bottle of beer for him.

"No time like the present, eh, Mr. Archer? What about bearding Fairbrother in his den tonight?"

"Suits me, Squire."

"Right, I'll give him a ring as soon as we get back and fix an appointment."

Before they moved off for the afternoon Tom had a chance to take his brother-in-law aside. "Worth having a go to try to keep all this lot, isn't it, Dan?" The sweep of his arm took in the Manor estate. "Won't be any need for a gamekeeper if the ironstone lark gets going. I'll lose my job more than likely." He nudged Dan in the ribs and gave him a lop-sided grin. "You and Doris don't want to keep me for the rest of my born days, do you?"

At the end of the day when the bag was split up and each man received a pheasant, a brace of partridge, a hare and a rabbit, Tom noted with satisfaction there were thirty birds, seven hares and a couple of dozen rabbits left to help pay the maintenance cost of the shoot.

There was also a solitary woodcock. The stocky gamekeeper glanced around the group of men, looking for the missing pin-feather he knew would be tucked in somebody's hatband. Dan Archer had it. Tom gave him his warm, slow smile. No man who sported a woodcock feather would abandon his shooting without a devil of a fight.

VI

THE oak-panelled hall of the Manor where Dan Archer stood waiting for the Squire that evening was lofty and dignified. It was not so highly polished as it used to be in more spacious days. The carved crests carried a light film of dust and here and there snuff-like yellowy grains betrayed the presence of woodworm. The Squire reflected, as he went to greet Dan, that his mother would never have tolerated that; but then, in her day, domestic servants were not so hard to come by or so dear to keep.

Lawson-Hope wondered how many of Dan's ancestors had stood waiting for his own forebears, as Dan stood waiting for him now. Dozens, he supposed. For centuries both families had played their quiet part in the village with nothing much to show for it, except perhaps their monuments in the village cemetery and the wholesomeness of the lives they had taught their sons and daughters to lead.

"This way, Mr. Archer. Let's have a drink before we go up there, what?" The Squire led the way into his lounge, conscious that it was a little shabby. The old leather armchairs were getting worn, the head of a stag above the mantelpiece was grey and mottled with age. The book-cases round the walls were filled with Victorian three-volume novels. Nowadays the Squire had little time for reading and he had not bought a book for years. On a table beside his chair was a pile of *Country Life*, and an unopened copy of the morning's

Times. Unless there was grave news of crises in politics the Squire kept his papers for Sunday and went through the six of them in the morning, after his dutiful appearance at the village church.

In the crystal decanters on a side table, in the hunting cups carefully polished on the mantelpiece and in the precious china kept behind glass doors there were memories of a more leisurely age. Lawson-Hope heaved a sigh of regret at the passing of the Edwardian era and settled Dan in an armchair with a stiff whisky.

"Dashed awkward, what?" he said, meaning nothing in particular. It was his way of opening a conversation in which he wanted the other man to do most of the talking.

"I wonder, Squire," said Dan, "if we'll ever get people like Fairbrother to understand."

"Can't think why the Government doesn't intervene," said Lawson-Hope, scowling. For the last fifty years, every successive government had disappointed him a little more than the one before.

"Governments only remember us folk when there's a war on," said Dan. "Most of the time those chaps in Whitehall muck us about all ways, chopping and changing. In the war it was grain crops. Then it was milk. Then it was pigs. Then, blow me if they didn't shift the subsidies over to beef. Chop, change and muck about without giving you time to turn round. Do they think the land comes in three storeys, one for crops, one for cows and sheep, and the top one for hens and pigs?"

The Squire was only half listening, for his mind still harked back to a romantic, idealised picture of Merrie England when knights and their attendant squires rode through the wide green forests and caught their own venison and fish from the well-stocked woods and streams. In those days the cities were small and the air all over the shires and towns was sweet to breathe. Those were the days that would never be recaptured, the days of knight errantry, witchcraft, laughing orange girls, and fair ladies for whom a man would willingly risk his life at the point of a sword. In those days every man had been his own poet, and all men had stood upright and unafraid. Few reminders of those spacious days remained, but he believed that what little still existed had to be preserved. He would not stand idle while the last of the green fields were torn up to make a new Jerusalem for ironmongers.

"We must make that fellow understand," insisted the Squire, clutching his glass tightly.

As they drove the short distance to Fairbrother's farm, Lawson-Hope talked of restocking the trout stream and planting some new trees. "I think poplars instead of willows this time. Might have a bit of trouble rearing 'em in the early stages, but they should be worth it in the years to come." He hoped he was giving the sturdy farmer sitting beside him a reassuring sense of continuity and calm. By planting trees for the next generation, Lawson-Hope was making an act of faith in the future. Ironmongers may come and go, but the love of sunlight and shade beside the speckled river went on for ever.

The car turned into the gravel drive at the back of Fairbrother's house and Grace greeted them at the door. Surprised to see how pale and drawn she looked, the Squire enquired after her health. She gave him a tight, wistful smile, protesting she was feeling fine, but he noticed she hurried them along to her father's study as though she did not wish to be questioned too closely.

After the first formal greeting, Fairbrother leaned against his desk and, head on one side, eyed his visitors expectantly. Lawson-Hope cleared his throat.

"Look here, Fairbrother—about this confounded ironstone business——"

"Yes?"

"We'd like to know what's going on, Mr. Fairbrother," Dan said. "I'm afraid the farmers are a bit restive, not knowing what the future's likely to be— or if there's any future at all for 'em."

Fairbrother still seemed disinclined to speak and Lawson-Hope hurried to fill the silence.

"I needn't tell you, Fairbrother, how much we all deplore the firing of your ricks. That was an act of wanton damage——" His voice trailed off as Fairbrother made a gesture of irritation.

"A sign of how far behind the times Ambridge is, Squire. That's Industrial Revolution stuff. Puts me in mind of the ancient earthy clods who burnt the ricks and broke up the machines rather than admit that the inexorable tide of industrial progress had blunted their scythes and changed their way of life."

"Maybe." Dan leaned forward and knocked out his pipe on the grate. "But that doesn't get us very far. We farmers would like to know what's going to happen—when it pleases you to tell us."

"There's my answer!" snapped Fairbrother abruptly, pulling open a desk drawer and waving a sheaf of papers before him. "There's a draft agreement between Crawford and myself over the mineral rights to the Manor estate. He's coming in with me on the deal." He waited for the information to sink in, his cold gaze examining their surprised faces, before he went on in his precise, dry tones: "He's a business man of plain common sense, the type who has made this country what it is in the world today. Due for a knighthood, perhaps, twelve months hence. He's not living in the past and befogged by stupid sentimentality. He's a big man—a really big man, and you're only going to annoy him if you go on vaguely about people having lived here for so many years in the same old rut. Change is good for all of us."

He tossed the document back in the drawer and closed it with a decisive slam.

"One or two clauses aren't quite final, but when they're settled, Crawford will sign, be sure of that. He knows a good thing when he sees it. Furthermore, I've made our applications to the Ministry of Town and Country Planning. As soon as we get permission we start mining."

"You will mine against the express wish of the whole district." Lawson-Hope's voice was low. He felt old, incapable of stemming the drive of the energetic, determined man who stood wide-legged before him.

"From the way the people have damaged my property and tried to wreck my farm I don't think the men of Ambridge have paid much consideration to me. Why should I bother about them?" Fairbrother asked. "We go ahead, Squire, with or without the goodwill of Ambridge."

Fairbrother must have sensed the frustration of the old man, for his manner relaxed and a cynical smile played around the corners of his lips. He waved Dan to help himself to tobacco from the jar on the table, but the farmer shook his head and slowly got to his feet.

Lawson-Hope caught the farmer's eye. Dan's glance said plainly there was nothing more they could do, but the Squire was loath to give up.

"Why has Crawford paid us only one visit?" he asked.

Fairbrother said: "He's a very busy man!"

"Perhaps it is superfluous to ask if it's too late to change your mind?"

"Much, much too late."

Sadly, silently, Lawson-Hope allowed Dan to lead him to the study door. He paused for a moment as though to say something further, but could not think coherently. He found himself sitting in his car and Dan climbing in beside him before he realised he had passed young Grace in the hall without saying good-night.

"How did it go, Daddy?" Grace stood in the front porch watching the car move away slowly down the drive.

"Couple of old fools," her father said, coming in and closing the door.

"Do we really need any more money, Daddy? Do we need to dig up that beastly iron? Can't we leave Ambridge in peace?"

"Business is not for little girls to worry about." He put his arm across her shoulder. "While I live, Grace, you won't want for anything. That's all you need to be sure about."

She edged away from his arm. "I don't want money. Only—only——" Her voice trailed away to silence, and, with a hopeless shrug, she went upstairs to bed.

VII

IT was a raw Sunday night early in November and, cloaked in the darkness as she walked home from church, Christine Archer went over in her mind the events of the past fortnight.

The Squire seemed to have done nothing since his abortive meeting with Fairbrother a couple of weeks ago and she became so absorbed in wondering about the future of the village that it was some time before she realised someone was following her. She glanced over her shoulder, but it was too dark to see anything, though she guessed from the sound it was a man's tread.

A wave of cold air swept through the main street and, shivering, she turned up her coat collar to cover the tips of her ears. Gripping her prayer-book more firmly, she quickened her pace again. So did the man behind her.

He whistled her, but she hurried on, conscious that he was steadily overtaking her. She was determined to avoid breaking into a run that might betray her alarm.

A quarter of an hour ago there had been a few people around when the congregation went home after evensong; now Ambridge village street seemed deserted. Christine regretted she had stayed chatting to her sister-in-law, Peggy, at the lych gate instead of going home with her father and mother.

At last the follower was on top of her. She tried not

to look round. A momentary feeling of panic brought a flutter to the muscles of her throat.

"Hey, what's the hurry, then?"

She recognised the voice as belonging to Bill Slater, her father's young hired hand. Her panic died down and she paused, but there was something in his tone that left her with a feeling of uneasy tension.

"Hullo, Bill," she said evenly. "I didn't know it was you."

"Where are you going?" he asked, moving closer. His overcoat smelt of stale tobacco.

"Home." She saw the pale smudge of his face moving in the darkness as he walked beside her with the nervous, hurrying tread of the townsman.

"You don't want to go home yet."

The flutter came back to her throat. She remembered his glances when they met around the farm, the way he watched her get on her bicycle every morning to ride to work, the angry embarrassment she felt when his eyes were on her, bold, suggestive, brazen.

She turned to walk on, but after a couple of paces he caught her arm and brought her to a standstill, facing him.

"What d'you want?" she snapped, annoyed at the touch of his thin hand on her arm.

"Be a sport," he said. "Come on. No one need ever know."

She was frightened and angered by the familiarity of his tone. He tried to slip his arm around her waist, but she twisted away. The smell of tobacco was odiously close, and she could hear his quick and eager breathing.

"Bill, don't be an idiot!" It was the wrong thing to say, she realised too late.

"What's the matter with me?" He shoved his face

close. The smell of beer almost nauseated her. "No need to be hoity-toity 'cos I work for your dad. Things would be different if he worked for me."

"You've been drinking again!" she said in disgust.

"Come for a walk. Just a little walk. Won't take you far."

"No."

"Come on, be a sport, be a sport." His tone was whining and reiterative, like that of a spoiled child.

"I'm going home!"

She turned away swiftly, but again he caught her arm. She tried to shake herself free, but his grip was to strong. His other arm reached around her back. It was thin, hard and cold. It did not feel like flesh to her, but like the branch of some fantastic tree in a nightmare forest.

"Let go, Bill! Let me go!"

"I'm walking you home, see, whether you like it or not."

"I don't want you to, thanks." The pressure on her arm increased and he tried to pull her towards him. The pitch of her voice rose. "Bill! Stop it! Let me go!"

She saw he was trying to drag her to the small iron gate leading to the bridle-path across the fields. Angrily she wrenched herself free with a sudden twist beneath his arms. In a flash his chilly arms were round her and she was pinned against the gate, almost sick with the pain of the sharp iron pressing into her backbone.

"Bill—you're hurting!"

He held her tighter, his whole weight keeping her back against the gate, and tried to trap her lips. Her arms were crushed against his chest and she again tried to push him away, twisting and turning her head to escape from the menace of his lips.

"Leave me alone! Get away from me! Please, Bill, please!"

He gave up the attempt to kiss her face. Unexpectedly, his mouth was wet on her neck. She screamed at his touch.

"Shut up, you little fool," he whispered, as if they were in a conspiracy together.

Her heart hammered with rage and fear. Even as she struggled she realised that she had not the strength to get away.

Suddenly another figure appeared out of the darkness. A gnarled hand fastened on Bill's unruly hair and jerked his head back. A yelp of pain was forced from him and his grip on Christine slackened at last. A shove sent him spinning against the railings with a jolt.

"Young rapscallion!"

Relief filled Christine at the sound of old Walter Gabriel's voice. She leant against the railings, striving to control the trembling which seemed suddenly to possess her from head to foot.

"Varmint!" Walter's hands fastened on the lapels of Bill's overcoat and shook him like a rat. "I'll give you, molestin' her!"

"He's drunk, Walter," Christine panted. "Drunk."

"Oh, is he!"

Bill tried to twist out of Walter's grasp, but the old man held him firmly.

"You all right, Christine?"

"Yes, Walter." The trembling was easing now.

"Right. Come on, me lad. We'll soon settle you."

Walter broke the silence only once in the hundred

yards to Mrs. Perkins' cottage. "If it wasn't for me respect for your auntie I'd give you a damn good thrashin', young feller."

Christine did not want to go in, but Walter took complete charge. He brushed aside the questions of the tall, angular woman who opened the door, marched Bill out to the back kitchen, shoved his head under the cold tap and held him there. "That ought to dampen his ardour."

"What's he been up to now?" Mrs. Perkins folded her arms across her bony body and turned to Christine. "Drinking again?"

Although she had never been out of Greater London until she moved to Ambridge, Mrs. Perkins had the desiccated look of a woman who had lived for years in the tropics. Hands and forearms were bony, capable, swarthy as a gipsy's. There was a faintly forbidding air about her. She consciously and frequently adopted the pose of a craggy martinet—a pose given away by the lively shrewdness and warmth of her brown, darting eyes and the kindliness of her features when she was not trying to look severe.

She stood waiting for an answer, but Christine avoided her eyes, shook her head and said nothing, unwilling that the old woman should see she had been through an emotional storm.

Looking at Bill standing at the sink, head down, sullen, ashamed yet glowering, Christine realised with a shock how he had changed in the past few months.

She remembered his arrival in Ambridge, pale and weak, but clean, bright-eyed and willing. He had a chest ailment aggravated by the stale air of the soot-ridden factory in which he worked near London. It was on the river where, for many months of the year, the mists gave the smog no chance to dissipate. "All I want is an open-air job and a chance to get well," he had told Dan Archer.

Then there had been talk around the family table, while he had been making up his mind.

"I want more help, but I want a strong lad, not a blessed semi-invalid," Dan Archer had said.

However, largely because Bill was Mrs. Perkins' nephew and a kind of cousin by marriage, he yielded to the family and took him on.

The open-air life did the boy good—for a while. As often as he could manage it, he would be at the wheel of the tractor, for his interest in farming was related to his handiness with machines. But his interest did not last. There was nothing in him that gave him a natural affinity with the countryside. The Archer family were soon aware that he was ill at ease in Ambridge. Only the risk to his health kept him from returning to metropolitan Essex and all that went with it.

Christine had watched his losing struggle to adjust himself to his environment and his growing discontent at the realisation that he was not one of them. Then had come a series of almost childish attempts to assert himself and, when they failed, a sourness and surly indifference to the people around him. It was only when he started gambling and drinking with a crowd of village youths as weak-willed and feckless as himself that he found something to bolster his ego. He felt more and more important as his pitch-and-toss winnings and liquor consumption increased. A big frog in a little pool, Christine reflected—and the pool itself was stagnant.

Now, standing at the sink, his mouth sagging and eyelids drooping, he looked far older than his twenty years. His complexion was muddied and there was a dissipated look around his eyes. His mousy hair was dull and hung unkempt over his forehead.

"Get to bed!" Walter snapped, moving towards the basin.

The boy went without looking at any of them.

"Now, what's he been up to?" Mrs. Perkins asked again.

Walter told her, not sparing the details. Once Christine looked at him appealingly, but he waved her objections aside.

Mrs. Perkins tried to say something in apology for her nephew.

"Forget it," Christine said uncomfortably. "Please forget it."

"No. That young feller's got to be taught a lesson." Walter stood determinedly in front of the fire. "Been going from bad to worse lately, ma'am, though I hates to say it. Boozing, gambling and quarrelling summat cruel."

Mrs. Perkins nodded.

"I know that only too well, Mr. Gabriel," she said in her sepulchral tones. "Dunno what's got into him. He used to be a nice boy, but lately . . ."

"Damn young scamp." Walter fingered the buckle of the heavy leather belt that had held his stomach up for the last twenty years. There was a determined gleam in his watery eyes. "Deal with him if you like, ma'am?"

Mrs. Perkins shook her head, the lines of her mouth set firm.

"I'll deal with him," she said quietly. "Just wait till

he gets the edge of my tongue. If he doesn't mend his ways I shan't have him under my roof."

"Dunno what your father's going to say about this, Chris," Walter wheezed with gloomy satisfaction. "Sack him like as not. Serve him right, too. He got in with the wrong crowd. He's been warned often enough."

Christine could imagine her father's anger—and the complications if Bill were sacked. The boy was too closely associated with the family—a nephew of Mrs. Perkins, a cousin of Peggy, her brother Jack's wife.

"Dad won't know anything about it," she said quietly. "Not from me, anyway."

Walter's wrinkled face was incredulous, but Mrs. Perkins shot her a quick look of gratitude and understanding.

"And you needn't say anything, Walter. I'm grateful you came along when you did." Christine coloured a little and looked appealingly at the older woman. "As far as I'm concerned it's over and done with, Mrs. P. Couldn't we forget it?"

"It won't happen again," Mrs. Perkins said. "I'll see to that." She fetched the kettle, filled it and glanced formidably up at the ceiling. "Let him wait and wonder what's coming to him. Do him good to be left up there on his own to think a bit."

They had a cup of tea together and Walter insisted on walking back up to Brookfield with Christine.

"The good lady's got a scathin' tongue when she wants to use it," he rasped. "But I'm thinkin' it'll take more than words to show young Bill the error of his ways."

He left her at the gate at Brookfield, but his voice came back to her through the orchard.

"Wants a good hidin'. Get some young feller to give him one. Goo'night."

As she crossed the yard, Christine reflected that it was becoming dangerous to be outside at night in Ambridge. She recalled what had happened two nights ago; she had been crossing the fields to call for Phil at his office, and thought she had heard rustling in the hedge behind her.

As she and Phil had walked home, she had told him of the noise and the pair of them had walked quietly towards the trout stream. A light showed up among the drilling equipment and, sensing trouble, they had hurried over. Somehow the intruders must have realised they were discovered, for they raced off before Phil and Christine could reach the drill.

It did not take long to discover the diamond drill-head and the drilling rods had been stolen.

"Sabotage again," Phil had said. "Aimed at the heart of the trouble this time."

Christine wondered who could be so desperate as to interfere in such a manner. To outsiders the most obvious suspects were Phil and Jane. Beyond and within her own circle of relatives Christine could find no one individual who would be guilty of such an action. But if she thought about it dispassionately, she was forced to conclude that the damage must have been done by one of the tenant farmers who was directly affected by the new scheme.

But which one?

When she got into the house the kitchen was empty, but there was a light in the sitting-room, as there always was on Sunday night. Christine stopped at the hall mirror long enough to make sure she was tidy, straightened her hair where Bill had ruffled it and, composing herself, went in.

Phil and Jane were together on the settee, but for once they were not working. Scribbled notes and papers were laid aside at their feet. Dan Archer was at his old roll-top walnut desk half-heartedly doing his booking; her mother sat in an armchair by the fire, steel knitting needles busily clicking their way through a pair of socks.

Phil gave a broad grin, winked at Jane and moved over to make room for his sister by the fire.

Dan slapped down some papers with an exclamation of annoyance and turned to look at his family. His eye caught an amused expression on Jane's face.

"It's all right for you to laugh, my lass," he said. "But you don't have to fill in all these blessed forms like I do."

"All in a good cause," Jane said, trying to hide her smile.

"D'you know what I'd do if I was Minister of Agriculture?" Dan said after a few moments. "I'd take all the officials and choke 'em with their own paper. Then I'd shoot myself. At least I'd know I'd done some good for my country."

The laughter faded when Phil got up from the settee and stirred the untidy spread of papers at his feet.

"You might include Fairbrother and Crawford in your purge, Dad. Then you'd be doing something even better for agriculture."

Doris stopped knitting.

"Anything fresh about this Mr. Crawford yet?"

Dan grunted and stretched himself. The upright chair creaked under his weight.

"Nobody knows what Fairbrother's been up to since Squire and I saw him last, any more than anybody knows where the diamond drill-head is. That saboteur has been mighty busy lately." He reached for his pipe. "Police haven't got anybody for pinching it yet, have they?"

"Don't think so," Phil replied. "Uncle Tom found the last of the missing drill-rods in the reeds by the trout stream this morning, but nobody's turned up the drill-head."

Fairbrother had informed the police immediately Phil told him of their discovery that someone had been tampering with the drilling equipment.

The following morning there had been great excitement, with a detective over from Borchester who had tested for fingerprints around the mineralogist's lorries. He found nothing of significance.

Police spent some time interviewing people in the village without success, but the drill-rods, which had been scattered throughout the fields, were gradually recovered, one or two each day.

Drilling work was still held up until a new diamond drilling-head was brought from London. Grace was due to bring it back next day, after spending the week-end with friends.

"The drill-head was worth about fifty pounds." Phil ran his hand through his curly hair and scratched the back of his head, a gesture he had learnt from Dan. "What with the rick fire and the sheep that had to be destroyed, the saboteurs are running up a tidy bill for Fairbrother."

"I feel like a criminal every time I go outside the door," Doris said. "It's terrible to walk down the village street now. Everybody's suspect—and it'll be like that until whoever's responsible is caught."

"What beats me is that there's folk in Ambridge daft enough to believe that damaging Fairbrother's property is any solution," Dan said.

They talked around it for an hour or more during which Christine found that, rather than listening, she was studying Phil and Jane. She noticed the quick understanding there was between them and the natural way they seemed to complement each other in their mutual interest in salvaging what they could of their employer's farm. But, like Doris, she did not trust that red hair and that wide, curled mouth.

Next morning Christine saw Bill Slater again.

She was pushing her bicycle through the yard, but he did not meet her glance. He slipped quickly away out of sight into the barn and her heart lightened as she mounted her cycle and rode off, knowing that for once his brazen gaze was not following her.

Somehow the day's work seemed to go much easier and quicker and that evening when she left the milk depôt and saw Grace Fairbrother waiting in her car outside, she was genuinely pleased to see her.

"Just got home from London with the new drill-head and thought you might like a lift as I was passing," Grace explained. "Haven't seen you lately, Chris. When are you coming over for a meal?"

"Any time you like," said Christine. She tied her bicycle to the rack behind the car and got in beside Grace.

Grace took a corner swiftly but carefully before she answered. "Not tomorrow, anyway. A fellow called Crawford is coming and I don't think you would like him much."

"Thanks for the warning," said Christine. "What you've just said isn't confidential, is it?"

Grace smiled wryly. "Whoever heard of secrets between women?"

By the time they reached Ambridge it was dark and cold. The windows of the cottages were shuttered, and there was no sound but the mournful creak of ancient trees flanking the deserted village street. Grace shuddered as she let Christine out of the car.

"Like a ghost town already, isn't it?"

Christine overtook her mother going into the house from the dairy with a jug of milk for tea.

"Tell your father and Phil, Chris," Doris said when she heard her news. "It may spoil their tea, but it's better they should know."

"Crawford arrives tomorrow," Chris announced the moment she got in the kitchen.

"What?" Dan looked up from his newspaper. "What did you say?"

"Crawford arrives tomorrow. That's all I know. I don't know if he has his pick and shovel with him or not. I don't know if he's bringing in a squad of men with lamps on their heads or not. I only know he's coming."

While her father and brother looked at her dumbfounded, her mother went on placidly setting the kitchen table. Doris held the firm belief there was no situation so grave that it should be allowed to upset regular meal-times.

"Come on, everybody—tea."

Dan asked, "How did you find out, Chris?"

"Grace told me to tell you." She felt no harm would be done by a slight embroidering of the truth.

"That's something, anyway," said Phil.

"Eat up, Dan," said Doris, and he did as he was told, taking rather longer than usual over his meal because he was thinking aloud, with occasional help from Doris or Christine, about what this new development would mean.

The family sat around the kitchen table long after tea was finished speculating about Crawford, until, with an air of determination, Dan got up and put on his overcoat.

"I'm going to see the Squire," he said. "He might be able to have a chat with Crawford and make him see what a tragedy it'll be if ironstone comes to Ambridge."

"If he's going to do any good he'll have to be quick about it," Doris said. "He didn't do much good with Fairbrother himself."

"Just what I was thinking." Dan reached for his hat. "The Squire will have to talk before Crawford signs over the mineral rights."

Christine was in the bathroom doing her hair when Phil came upstairs to change for his Young Farmers' Club meeting.

"Don't go away for a minute. Want to talk to you," she said determinedly.

He glanced at his watch and waited with amused tolerance until she arranged her hair to her satisfaction.

"I drove back from Borchester with Grace today," Chris said when she turned from the mirror. Her face was serious. "She looked pretty unhappy to me."

"Is that my fault?" He avoided her eyes.

"Perhaps not entirely. But she's getting a lean time of it. Phil—don't you think you could be a bit more friendly towards her?"

Phil shrugged his shoulders and kicked lightly at a crumbling corner of the cork bath-mat.

"Seems that every time we speak to each other now we start fighting," he said. "I don't think we mean to. It just happens."

"At least she was open about Crawford coming tomorrow. She didn't *have* to say anything about it." Christine went to the bathroom door. "She made the gesture to us. Somebody ought to let her know we are grateful."

VIII

PHIL washed and changed, turning Christine's words over in his mind. The shrewd countryman in him knew that if there was one person capable of persuading Fairbrother against going ahead with the ironstone scheme, it was Grace. But what had she to gain if she did?

Throughout the evening his thoughts kept returning to her. A few weeks ago they were both happy with each other. She was his girl; everything was settled. Now all was different. If they could get back on their old footing he knew he might give her the strength to oppose her father. He toyed with the idea of putting up a pretence, but . . .

After the Young Farmers' Club meeting Phil spent a few minutes in the smoke-laden bar at the Bull, enjoying the insults Walter Gabriel and Simon hurled at each other over a game of crib. Walter broke off long enough to say:

"Heard as you was interested in rentin' some grass keep, Phil."

"That's right."

"Got to know about three lots in market today." Walter paired Simon's card and pegged himself two points with a triumphant chuckle. "Tell you about 'em when I've dusted Simon off."

Eventually Walter finished his game. Eventually, also, with many a wink, grimace and digression, he parted with the names of the farmers with pasture to spare.

"I'll look into it, Walter," Phil said. "Thanks."

There were so many things to do around Fairbrother's farm that it was not until late the following morning, while he was looking over some store cattle and discussing their diet with the cowman, that he remembered the pasture again.

"Must do something about that grass keep—now," he muttered. "See you later."

He left the yard and made his way around the outbuildings towards the farm office. A sound in the stables made him stop at the door and look in.

Grace, in slacks and loose overall, was busy grooming her horse. Her jet-black hair was tousled and there was hardly any make-up on her face.

Her lack of elegance, whether or not it was purposeful, emboldened Phil. She was not after all a being on a pedestal. She was human, like himself, lovelier than most people, with only that flintish father to love her. Phil had never imagined her as the centre of a laughing crowd, because he had never seen her in a crowd. Perhaps she needed him to share her isolation.

From the door he looked across to her, to the jet hair, the pale face, the dark lashes over her unhappy eyes. He looked hard at her straight nose and at the firm, curving mouth, before he walked quietly across the straw litter and around to the other side of the mare.

She did not hear him come in and carried on with her grooming, talking and cooing softly to the horse. Phil watched her until her awkwardness with the brush under its belly made him move towards her.

"No, Grace," he said in a friendly tone. "Like this."

His shoulder and back muscles rippled as he worked rhythmically with the brush. She stood close, admiring his quick, efficient movements that brought an almost metallic gloss to the horse's coat.

"I'll give her a run this morning," said Grace thankfully. "Show off her beautiful shine to all the neighbours."

He straightened up and their eyes met. Absently he cupped his hand for the mare to nuzzle, remembering what Christine had told him.

"Will you have time? I thought——" He stopped, suddenly uncertain of himself.

"Yes?"

"Oh—nothing important," he mumbled.

"Mr. Crawford doesn't arrive until later in the day—if that's what you're thinking."

Her voice was frank and for a moment Phil was conscious of a return of the easy confidence that used to exist between them.

"Smashing crystal ball you've got," he said smiling.

"It doesn't give all the answers, though," she said wistfully.

He saw the signs of worry round her eyes and sympathy for the girl welled up in him. She looked away self-consciously and tried to smooth her tumbled hair.

"I look a mess."

"You look perfectly all right to me."

The gentleness in his voice seemed to kindle a responsive warmth in her. The tight little lines around her mouth disappeared, her lips parted in a grateful smile and her features softened.

Deep instinct in them reached out, beating down the recent barriers that had grown up between them.

The old yearnings came back to Phil. He knew that if he could take her in his arms now, at this moment, and kiss her, he would feel her lips responding to him as they had in the past. . . .

The mare whinnied and stirred restlessly and he had to step back to avoid a pawing hoof. Dropping the brush he looked again at Grace, seeing the appeal in her eyes as she waited for his arms and the closeness of him to wipe out the loneliness of the past weeks. But the horse lunged forward and he had to step back again.

A hot, sharp pain stabbed into his shoulder and he felt his coat sleeve rip on a nail.

"Hell!"

The word burst from his lips. He wrenched himself free and clouted the nail hard with the heel of his hand.

Unmindful of the blood spurting where the nail had ripped his hand, he swung round, but as he turned he knew the spell was broken. Grace's attention was on the restless, snorting mare.

Uncertain and loath to accept that the mood could not be recaptured, but aware that the ephemeral communion was gone, he found himself saying, "She wants more exercise."

Grace insisted on getting a plaster for his hand. He wandered out of the stable and waited for her at the door of the farm office, watching one or two of the employees going about their work in the yards. When he came back he noticed she had found time to run a comb through her hair.

"Sorry about that nail, Phil." Her voice was cool, with a note of challenge. He could only see the top of her shining head as she bent over his hand, pressing the plaster firmly into his palm, and he wondered if there was hidden meaning in what she said.

"Not half so sorry as I am." His words sounded inadequate, but his own reserve had returned. "Hope it isn't going to be a difficult day for you, Grace."

"A lot depends on how difficult I want to make it." She continued to busy herself with the plaster and he could feel her hands trembling. "I think, if I wanted to, I could spoil Daddy's day for him." The words were soft, almost whispered.

Do it. Do anything to put Crawford off. The words raced through his mind, but the barriers were up again. They were in opposite camps with the fields of ironstone between them, in spite of her warm fingertips on his hand.

She released him suddenly.

"Don't go hanging yourself on nails again. It—it's very destructive."

He smoothed the plaster on his palm with his thumb as she walked away, back to the house. An impulse to follow her prompted him, but he knew the eyes of the workmen in the yard were on him. He caught a last glimpse of her before she entered the house, then turned abruptly and strode across to his farm truck.

Driving around the farm lands, his interest returned gradually to his work. Phil believed in the old saying that the best manure the land could have was a farmer's boot. He trusted his workmen but at the same time liked seeing for himself how the work was going.

The truck bounced along at a fair pace, but there was little that missed Phil's sharp eyes. He saw the margin of a field of greens that had been eaten off by rabbits, and mentally traced the culprits to a couple of large burrows well hidden among the nettle beds.

"Time those nettles died off," he thought. "There's a couple of Sunday mornings' ferreting there when you can see what you're shooting at. When the mist has gone, I'll get round to it."

He pulled up at the gate of the ley where Jane Maxwell, with an old pony, was hauling the regular lines of poultry fold-units on to fresh ground. He noted with satisfaction the draught-board pattern of rich grass coming through where the birds had scratched and foraged a week or two before.

He was on the point of stopping, but the sudden pressure of the cut in his palm on the steering wheel made him content to pass by, exchanging a friendly wave with the girl.

He spent the rest of the morning weighing and selecting pigs for the bacon factory. Then, after dinner, he drove around the district to see the farmers Walter Gabriel had recommended to him the previous evening. By the time he got back to the farm office in the middle of the afternoon he was impatient and irritable.

Jane looked up from the order she was writing for poultry food.

"What on earth——!"

"Grass-keep to rent!" Phil snorted. "Pasture to rent!"

"Wasn't it any good?"

"Good! It was perfect! But can we get it? Hah!" He poked furiously at the coke stove and opened the damper. "Not a ghost of a chance."

"What happened?"

He moved over to the desk and hitched his leg on it.

"The same old story. I said I was interested. They said they were glad, *but*—was it for my father or was it

95

for Fairbrother? When I said Fairbrother, out came the excuses and apologies."

"In fact," Jane said, "as far as the local farmers are concerned, there's no keep to let to our lord and master."

"Right. Since the ironstone business there's not one of 'em would lift a finger to help him out of a hole. Can't say I blame 'em, but it doesn't solve our problems."

Jane stretched and yawned.

"We can kiss some of the reorganisation plan good-bye, then," she said. "We'd worked on the basis of hiring keep. If we don't get it we'll be hopelessly over-stocked when Fairbrother starts getting the ironstone out."

Phil nodded.

"Then we'll have to think again," she said philoso-phically.

Her soft, undisturbed voice and the practicality of what she said dissipated Phil's irritation. Reluctantly, he smiled.

"You certainly take it as it comes, don't you?"

"What else is there to do?" She nodded significantly in the direction of the house. "Incidentally, Craw-ford's arrived."

"Heard anything?"

"Not a word." She opened a drawer, took out the reorganisation notes they had made together and fingered through them. "Yes, we'll have to think again. Shall we work on it tonight?"

"No need to drag you in. You'll get fed up with it." The wisps of her auburn hair danced crazily as she shook her head with exaggerated emphasis. Phil saw the hint of fatigue and strain in her face.

"You're tired, Jane. You're overdoing it." Besides, he did not want to be left alone with her, especially not tonight, which might well give him a chance to be reconciled to Grace.

She laughed unconvincingly. "I went to a dance last night, that's all."

He wondered sharply who had taken her, who she had danced with and how she had got home. Then the picture of Grace in the stable flashed into his mind and he cursed the confusion stirring in him. It was his bad luck to hunger for a woman in his arms when the wrong woman was flirting with him.

"I'll be here tonight," Jane was saying. "After all the work we've done together on the re-planning I want to see it through. And you needn't try to stop me."

She was there, true to her word, when Phil got back to the farm office after tea, sitting at the desk waiting for him. He did not know whether to be glad or sorry. She disturbed his senses alarmingly.

The atmosphere over the land was heavy, thunderous, and Phil was conscious of a feeling of something impending. It seemed to start in the stable with Grace that morning and had stayed with him all day—an uneasy restlessness of spirit that he could not wholly suppress.

Jane's expression was solemn and he waited for her to speak, wondering if her words would settle and pin down the confusion churning in the back of his mind.

"I've just come from the house," she said quietly. "They asked me in and gave me a drink. Everything was very convivial."

Phil offered her a cigarette. She took it and gave him a wan but faintly provocative smile.

"Everything seems to be going swimmingly—Fairbrother and Crawford bosom pals, Grace presiding like a benign goddess of plenty. It looks to me as though everything's settled. Fairbrother's as pleased as a cat with a saucer of cream."

She flicked a dead match into the grate, as if showing how little she approved of the dinner party, then went on.

"All along I've been hoping this re-planning of ours was all a waste of time. Now it looks as though it's not destined for the dustbin."

Phil was suddenly angry. His confusion cleared. He knew he had been waiting all day for Grace to help them—to do something that would put his work and the farm back into proportion, with ironstone a fading bad dream of the past. And she had done nothing. Nothing! Crawford and Fairbrother had had it all their own way.

Jane sat with her back to him, the curve of her shoulders plain through her blouse, the nape of her neck exposed where she leant forward over her scribbling pad.

Work! That was the thing. Work. At least it was understandable, predictable. At least it brought its rewards.

Almost fiercely Phil dragged up a chair and sat down beside the girl, forcing himself to forget his bitterness and disappointment and to concentrate on the planning tasks ahead.

"Start with the crop rotation." His tone was cold and businesslike. "Work out a crop plan and see how much stock we can expect to support on it."

He worked like a machine, unmindful of the passing of time or the increasing cold as the fire in the stove died down.

The metallic clatter of the coke hod broke through his indifference to his surroundings. Jane built up the fire and indulged herself in a noisy, uninhibited yawn.

She looked like a young child allowed to stay up long after its bedtime—dog-tired yet unwilling to admit it. Her hair was more unruly than usual where she had run her fingers through it time and again to keep herself alert. Her lids were heavy on her eyes and her chin trembled as she fought to stifle another yawn.

"Gosh, I'm sorry." Phil got up and reached for his coat. "I should have realised you were fagged out. Come on. I'll take you down to your digs."

"No, it's all right." She gave an apologetic smile. "You've not finished. I'll walk."

"You'll do nothing of the sort."

"I'm not going to drag you away. It's going too well."

He hesitated. He did not want to leave the office with Jane while he was waiting for Grace.

"Give me another half an hour? Yes?"

"Of course."

He glanced around the room, looking for somewhere comfortable for Jane to rest. In the corner were a couple of bales of new sacks. His knife went through the twine binding them and he spread them into a thick, soft mattress.

"Doss down there," he said absently.

She smiled her thanks, saying: "I'm a dead loss, aren't I?"

He rolled up a few more sacks to make a pillow and when she lay down thankfully, he threw his overcoat over her.

"I'll wake you when I've finished and run you home."

Phil went back to his work. He looked round once, saw she seemed to be sleeping, and he forgot about her in a tricky calculation of how much he could afford to cut down on his cash crops to provide more feed for his stock.

Estimates of next year's prices . . . estimates of the yield per acre . . . estimates of each animal's weekly consumption . . . labour . . . wages . . . man-hours . . .

When he looked at his watch again it was eleven o'clock. He sat at the desk for a while, soaking in the tranquil silence of the office, broken only by the regular breathing of the girl on the sacks behind him.

The uneasy restlessness he had kept at bay by occupying himself with work came back. He was too tired to grapple with it, unwilling to try and unravel this new awareness of his tangled emotions.

"You need an aspirin," he told himself, then smiled at his poor attempt to dismiss the matter.

Jane stirred under his overcoat, invisible but for her feet and a bunching crop of small curls over the coat collar.

He nudged her with his knee. She gave a sleepy sigh, rolled over and nestled more firmly into the sacks, one arm thrown back behind her head, the other across her body. She looked so peaceful it seemed a pity to disturb her. He stood quietly looking down at her, wondering if he should leave her.

In sleep she was lovely. The dull, coarse-meshed sacks enhanced her natural colouring, framed the serenity of her features.

Her lips moved. A drowsy, slurred syllable slipped from them and her eyelids flickered.

"Come on, sleepyhead."

He bent down, put an arm under her head to

help her to her feet and gently pulled back his over-coat.

The warm scent of her rose to him and he saw the rise and fall of her breast as she struggled back to conscious-ness. He felt his heart thudding.

Her lips moved again.

"Phil." It was little more than a drowsy sigh. She was still half asleep.

He held his breath, not daring to move.

"Phil . . . Oh, Phil."

Her arms were round him, insistent, urgent—and then she was fully awake, wide-eyed, staring up into his face a few inches from her.

For a moment he tried to break away, but the posses-sive grip of her arms did not slacken as she pulled him towards her.

He was drowsy, he had longed all day for Grace, his mind was uneasy, his spirit was desperately in need of consolation, and the sweet womanliness of her was al-most irresistible. For a second he hesitated, then he folded his arms around her back and closed his mouth across the soft and willing offering of her lips.

IX

THE DINNER had been a success—the success Grace Fairbrother had hoped for. She spent all day making sure that the cook knew exactly what she was doing with the freshly killed chicken, the mushrooms and the vegetables. Peaches had been brought from the larder and fresh cream from the dairy.

Her father had warned her that more business was done over a good meal than over an office desk. To a certain extent, she had played her part well—but suddenly she could act no longer. She felt that she must tell Crawford the truth, even if she humiliated and angered her father.

For a few minutes she was alone in the drawing-room, just long enough to concentrate her wavering courage.

"Will that be all, Miss Grace?"

Betty, the maid, paused at the door after clearing away the coffee things.

"Thank you, Betty."

From the study across the hall came the muted voices of Fairbrother and Crawford. The pungent scent of cigars crept through the house.

"I shouldn't bother to go into the study, Betty. They've just gone in there and won't want to be disturbed. But tell cook the dinner was very good. You both did well. My father was very pleased."

"Thank you, Miss Grace." The country girl smiled and was gone.

Left alone, Grace felt disappointed that she had let dinner pass without mentioning the Ambridge point of view. In her mind, she apologised to Phil.

There was her failure. She knew she had let him down. The promise she had made to herself that she would speak to her father, try to dissuade him from going on with the ironstone scheme, had never materialised. . . . Too many details of the meal and the room to be arranged, never a real opportunity to pin her father down before Crawford's arrival, and—cowardice?

Now dinner was over. The two men were discussing the details of the agreement on the mineral rights and she had said nothing.

In the empty room, she resolved to speak for Phil's sake and her own.

The strident ringing of the telephone through the quiet house brought her to her feet and out into the hall. Her voice was uncertain when she answered.

"Miss Fairbrother? It's Lawson-Hope."

"Good evening, Squire." What on earth did he want? she asked herself. The Squire normally refused to touch the telephone, which he regarded as an abomination.

"Hope I've not disturbed you. It's rather late . . ."

"That's all right," she replied, with the hint of a question in her voice.

There was a pause.

"The fact is——" The Squire seemed to be picking his words. "I wonder—would it be possible for me to have a word with Mr. Crawford?"

"Mr. Crawford!" She realised from his crisp affirmation she had sounded surprised. "Of course, Mr. Lawson-Hope. Just a moment. I'll fetch him."

A faint sign of irritation showed for a second on her father's face when she went into the study.

"Tell 'em I'll call 'em back, Grace. I'm busy just now." He had a pen and a sheaf of papers in his hand.

"It isn't for you, Daddy. It's for Mr. Crawford."

The papers scattered over the desk and on the floor before the fire told her the two men had been working hard to reach agreement on the ironstone scheme. Quietly she moved around the room, clearing the litter of cigarette and cigar ash from her father's desk, putting clean glasses with the decanter and exchanging the empty siphon for a full one. But she still had not sufficient confidence to plead with her father.

Crawford stuck his head round the corner of the door, an expression of amused bewilderment on his face.

"I've got an invitation to dine out tomorrow night, Fairbrother. Anything particular on? Don't want to clash with any arrangements you've made."

Fairbrother looked surprised and almost annoyed.

"Why, no. No—we've fixed nothing."

"Thanks." Crawford's head disappeared again as he returned to the telephone.

Grace could not avoid her father's eyes, which held hers at last.

"Who's on the phone?"

She faced him squarely, and pointed her chin high. "The Squire."

Crawford came back in, twirling the cigar in his fingers and studying the ash. Perplexed, his forehead wrinkled, he stood with his back to the log fire.

"Odd thing," he said thoughtfully. "That was your local squire. He's begged me not to sign away the mineral rights of the estate until he's had a chance to talk to me at dinner tomorrow night. Perhaps we had better put these papers away. He says he doesn't want this business to get as far as a public enquiry, which may be acrimonious."

Fairbrother turned his back and busied himself at the decanter. Grace thought his shoulders looked slumped and disappointed.

"He's a real old stick-in-the-mud," he said in a moment. "A die-hard."

"Really?" Crawford smiled to himself. "Doesn't sound such a peppery so-and-so as his cousin, the Colonel."

"Actually he's a bit of an old woman." Fairbrother came back to the fire and handed Crawford a stiff whisky. "Still a firm believer in the feudal system."

That's unfair, Grace thought. It's not true. He may be old-fashioned, perhaps a little quaint, but he's sweet and kind and chivalrous. She realised that by adopting a casual, half-jesting tone her father was deliberately playing down the effect of the scheme on Ambridge. Crawford, a stranger, could not be expected to know about it—unless she told him. He did not look perceptive enough to find out for himself. If she did not speak now she might never get another chance.

Fairbrother was looking at her. The meaning of his glance was obvious. He wanted her to go so that he could get to work again and persuade Crawford to sign.

Desperately she ignored him and forced herself to speak in the same light-hearted vein her father had used.

"Daddy's quite wrong, of course, Mr. Crawford," she smiled, hating herself for her duplicity. "The Squire just happens to think the same way as his tenants. He agrees with them that there's not much fun in the prospect of being ruined."

She had Crawford's ear. Those quiet, blue eyes of his were on her, studying her. No business man, she knew, wanted to ruin other men these days when the law was free to all and a man could have labour withheld from him if he made himself unpopular.

"Ruin? Nonsense!" There was an edge in Fairbrother's voice. "We've allowed for compensation. The people affected won't be out of pocket."

"But there is opposition, is there?" Crawford asked.

"Opposition!" Grace laughed mockingly. "The drill sabotaged—hayricks burnt down. We're all scheduled for a violent death in our beds——"

"The Industrial Revolution all over again," Fairbrother interposed promptly, in a voice of silk. "No amount of rioting managed to stop that. Er—they've only just heard about it in Ambridge, though. A bit late off the mark."

He stood up, tossed off his drink and eyed his daughter over the rim of his glass. He was, she thought, trying to give the impression that Ambridge was populated by violent and half-witted men and women.

"Whose side are you on, young lady?"

Grace realised that to Crawford her father's tone must still have sounded cordial, but she knew him better. The joviality with which it was delivered did nothing to soften the directness of the question.

She turned away, and, because she did not want to answer him directly, she changed the subject.

"You know, there's an awful fug in here. You'll be asphyxiated by cigar smoke if you work much longer in this atmosphere," she said, striving to make her tone casual.

Pulling back the curtains, she struggled with the window catch. Her father came over and helped her in silence. He did not look at her and she could sense his disapproval.

Across the drive a light was shining from the farm office. Once he had the window open, and the cool air began to blow in, Fairbrother glanced at his watch.

"Eleven o'clock, by jove, and Philip's still working." He looked back at Crawford. "My farm manager, you know. Nice young chap. Very capable—full of modern ideas." Taking Grace's elbow, he guided her firmly towards the door. "Go and ask him in for a drink, Grace. He certainly deserves one for working as late as this."

She went gratefully although knowing she had been sent out of the room deliberately so that her father could repair the damage she had done to his case.

Emotionally drained, she paused in the night air outside the back door, looking at the diamond-shaped stars glowing in the icy sky.

"Anyhow, I've spoken," she thought, hearing the scrape of a chair across the wooden floor of the farm office. "I can tell Phil now I haven't let him down." She felt that her conscience was clear and her spirits were peaceful.

Phil would never know what it had cost her to go against her father in front of Crawford. She prayed that he would understand, appreciate. . . . She walked across the dark yard hopefully.

Her thoughts went ahead of her footsteps into the farm office. Perhaps Phil would take her in his arms—as he had so nearly done that morning in the stable—and salve the loneliness she had suffered during the past weeks. They had been close together then; tonight the kindly darkness might help to complete their reconciliation.

Anticipation gripped her when she threw open the door of the farm office. Then the whole edifice of the future seemed to crumble around her.

She stared, horror-stricken, unbelieving.

Jane was half lying, half sitting on a pile of sacks in the corner. Beside her on one knee was Phil. His arms were round her, and his lips were tight across her mouth.

The sudden shock forced a gasp from Grace.

The couple separated, confused and dishevelled. She heard Phil's voice call to her as she turned to leave, but she had seen too much. She ran back to the house, guided more by instinct than by sight, for her eyes were blinded by a haze of tears, and she felt that she was alone in a world of mockery and pain.

X

THE VISITOR could see from the Bull register that remarkably few people stayed there in the course of a year. Nevertheless he allowed himself no misgivings and signed himself in, shivering in the icy draught that whipped under the front door and around the little hall table where he crouched, pen in hand. He felt he was a long way from his centrally heated university rooms in Iowa.

Cyrus J. Standish had hired a car in Borchester. In spite of the coldness of the night he had felt warm with anticipation as the chauffeur speeded towards the home of his ancestors. His enthusiasm was not even dampened by the driver's last comment, "Can't think what you want in this little place."

Yet Cyrus was somewhat disappointed as he carried his bag up to his room (nobody had offered to take it for him). He sat on the bed very gingerly and found that, as he expected, it was hard and lumpy. There was no heating in the room, so after unpacking a few things he went down to the bar where it was at least warm.

A rheumy-eyed man looked up from the wooden seat which ran along beside the brick fireplace. He nodded but did not speak, and Cyrus stood watching a group of villagers playing darts until he realised that in some way his scrutiny seemed to be disconcerting them. He moved to the bar and asked for a drink.

In the weeks since his arrival by air in Great Britain, Cyrus had visited the Arthurian sites in Cornwall and

Somerset, and had gone on to Oxford and Cambridge. In London he had familiarised himself with the landmarks and went on one of the five-hour tours of the capital which the agencies provide for tourists in a hurry. The city had been cosier and more intimate than he had expected. He had travelled up to Boston in Lincolnshire, to seek out the graves of some of his ancestors. From there he had continued to Coventry and Sheffield, because he felt that no picture of English life was complete without an impression of industrial strength and quality.

As Cyrus sipped a glass of rye whisky with which the proprietor, after some delay, had managed to provide him, he was able to look back on his weeks in Great Britain with some satisfaction.

He had found the churches and castles very small, the service in the hotels shocking and the goods in the stores of agreeable quality. Moreover, he liked the food and the people.

Oxford and Cambridge had disappointed him, because he considered them small and stuffy. The way the women undergraduates dressed filled him with astonishment when he remembered the co-eds on the campus at home. What other country but England would think of dressing eighteen-year-old girls in shapeless black suits and gowns?

The rheumy-eyed one moved from his corner seat and came to stand beside Cyrus.

"Getting cooler," he said affably in a voice of gravel.

"I hadn't noticed," said Cyrus. The other man seemed bemused and Cyrus remembered, too late, that the weather in England was an absorbing topic of conversation that must never be dismissed lightly.

Doggedly, the old man tried again.

"You be a stranger in these parts."

"Well, not exactly," said Cyrus. "You see, my mother's great-grandmother came from Ambridge, and I thought I'd come to see the place while I was over here."

"Fancy that," said the old man wonderingly. "Just fancy that. My old great-grannie, she's been dead and buried since the Boer War, near enough."

"Don't misunderstand me, sir," said Cyrus hastily. "She's dead enough, but I just might have relations here. My name is Cyrus Standish."

"I'm Walter Gabriel, and I can't recall as I ever met an American before, excepting for them gum-chewin' fellers what was over here in uniform during the last bust-up, and I ain't sure as you'd call them reg'lar Americans."

"Let's have a drink, shall we?"

"Well, sir, since you're kind enough to ask, 'twould be churlish of me to refuse."

The two men had several drinks before Cyrus elicited from Walter, whom he privately considered "a character", the information that the Squire, who made a point of studying old parish records to keep track of old-established families in the district, would be likely to know Cyrus's relatives. Gabriel himself said he had never heard tell of the Venn family about whom Cyrus was inquiring.

Standish was an informal and friendly fellow and decided to walk over to the Manor at once. He walked because he felt it was necessary to clear his head of the fumes of the landlord's inferior rye. On the way he whistled to himself a traditional English tune he had learnt recently and only stopped when he heard young, girlish voices in the darkness. He detected the trim outlines of two shadowy figures passing him on the roadway.

"Crawford's having dinner with him tonight and Dad's going up afterwards, Peggy," Cyrus heard one girl say.

"I don't know what to think about it, Chris," the other girl said. Cyrus noticed her accent was different—London, he thought.

"Jack says it'll be good for trade in the district, but I don't know. . . . It may bring a bit of life into the place, but will it be worth it?"

Cyrus disliked hearing snatches of conversation. His questing mind wanted to know what was said before and after. Times out of number his natural curiosity was frustrated, but tonight, with the thought of tracing his forebears uppermost in his mind, he would not allow himself to try and fit some coherent meaning to the remarks he had overheard.

It was a windy night and he walked quickly, aware that his head was beginning to ache abominably. He remembered that a seasoned traveller had once told him that it was always wise to drink "the wine of the country". So far he had found nothing in British beer to recommend it, but he resolved that the landlord of the Bull could keep his rye for more resilient customers.

His head filled with literary visions as he thought of the ancestors who had probably been along this same narrow road to the Manor. Were they squires, or knights, or gallant yeomen? Had they been the village vicars, or teachers?

Cyrus did not doubt for a moment that the Squire would be delighted to see him.

Chin up, Dan Archer submitted to his wife's inspection and allowed her to adjust his tie.

"That's better," Doris said, satisfied at last. "You mustn't go up to the Manor looking untidy."

"Squire's seen me in my working clothes often enough," Dan grunted. "It won't make any difference to him."

Doris turned his jacket pockets inside out, tut-tutting and clucking over the mess of fluff and tobacco shreds she shook out of the corners.

"Hurry up, love," the farmer said plaintively. "I'll be late."

She went round him briskly with a clothes-brush, stuffed a clean handkerchief in his pocket, stood back and surveyed him.

"Now you look quite nice, Dan."

"Quite sure you've done?"

He dragged on his mackintosh, rammed his trilby on his head, made sure his pipe and matches were in his pocket and moved to the door.

"Good luck, Dan. And don't you spare Mr. Crawford at all. You tell him."

"I'll speak my mind, Doris, don't you worry."

Driving up to the Manor Dan wondered what was in store. He had been wondering all day—ever since the Squire had rung up that morning.

"I'd like you to come up to the Manor after dinner tonight, Mr. Archer," Lawson-Hope had said. "I've persuaded Crawford to dine with me. We'll put our point of view to him this evening. Come about nine."

Dan parked his car under the magnolia tree on the edge of the lawn bordering the Manor drive. Clouds obscured the stars and he could tell from the feel of the breeze on his face that there was rain about.

He was admitted to the library, where Lawson-Hope and Crawford were discussing the scheme and drinking port. He liked the look of Crawford—a practical man, he thought—and was relieved to find the atmosphere cordial.

"I've asked Mr. Archer to come along because he's not directly affected by the ironstone scheme," the Squire explained. "He has no selfish motive, you understand. He just happens to be a farmer who hates to see good agricultural land ruined."

Dan gathered that the discussion had been going on some time. He sat back with a glass of beer, filled his pipe and listened, nodding from time to time as the Squire made a point. Crawford, he noticed, was listening attentively; he seemed to be the sort of man who liked to listen for a long time before he made up his mind.

When at last he did speak it was with quiet authority—a carefully marshalled, well-supported argument that knocked gaping holes in their case against the ironstone scheme.

"I must say," he wound up, "looking at it from the economic point of view——"

"Mr. Crawford, I've had the economic arguments dinned into my ears until I dream statistics." Lawson-Hope was on his feet and pacing around the room.

"I don't really see how you can argue with the facts," Crawford said reasonably.

"Facts and figures don't take into account the feelings of human beings, Mr. Crawford," Dan said. He could see that the Squire realised he was losing the argument.

Lawson-Hope shook a bony forefinger at Crawford.

"Tear the ironstone out of the land and you'll tear the heart out of the Ambridge people." He waved Crawford abruptly to silence when he made to reply. "The people's lives are wrapped up in the land—and that's how it's been for generations. The land's part of them."

"That's about the size of it, sir," Dan said. "We know these fields as well as we know our own kids— and what's more, we know how to treat 'em."

At this point, Cyrus J. Standish was announced by Lawson-Hope's wife, Letty. She was a well-meaning but vague woman whose head was so full of the business of different village committees and trying to run the Manor on a straitened budget that often she failed to appreciate what was going on around her. There had been a stranger in the house for dinner. Another stranger had arrived. Presumably they belonged together. She showed Cyrus into the library and promptly retired upstairs to her tussle with the Women's Institute balance sheet and her peppermints.

"I've come thousands of miles, sir, for the privilege of visiting this village," said Cyrus. "My folks came from these parts."

"Indeed," said the Squire, giving him a whisky. "Let me introduce Henry Crawford, a business man from the city, and Dan Archer, a tenant of mine."

Cyrus shook hands all round, smiling affably.

"Say now," he said, peering over his rimless spectacles at Crawford, "haven't I seen you before somewhere?"

"Maybe," said Crawford stiffly. "But there are a lot of people who look like me in this country."

"No, no, I've seen you before somewhere. I'll remember in a minute. You fellows just carry on—I'll ask you all afterwards what it is I want to know."

"Then if you'll permit me." The Squire turned to Crawford again. "There isn't much left in life these days that gives you a feeling of permanence. There are a few of us with our feet still buried in the soil, you might say, but we wouldn't be happy unless it was soil we knew and understood. An opencast mining scheme would alter the whole character of the land—and make a devil of a mess into the bargain."

Lawson-Hope moved to the old stone fireplace with the family coat of arms carved in the mantle. His finger traced out the deep-cut relief as he spoke and Cyrus's eyes gleamed with interest and awe.

"'This is the original bearing granted to William of Ambridge in the thirteenth century. This later addition here—the rose in the top quarter—was awarded to Black Sir Guy during the Wars of the Roses. Down here—this addition represents a musket ball. A Royalist Hope got that in the chest defending the Manor against a Roundhead siege."

Cyrus swallowed with delight at this evidence of tradition, but Crawford merely smiled.

"No autograph of Nell Gwynn?" the business man asked.

Lawson-Hope looked aggrieved. "I see you're not taking me seriously."

Crawford held his port up to the fire and examined the rich glow suffusing the glass. Then he said carefully:

"It seems to me a little insular—even selfish—when, for the sake of a past that's dead and gone, you wish to deprive the district of additional prosperity."

"There is such a thing as tradition," Dan said.

The American was pleased to hear Dan Archer speaking at last. It's all very well, Cyrus thought, for those with plenty of tradition to start chucking it away lightly as if it's a bundle of old straw. If they had none at all they would see how rootless and bewildered a community can be.

"But the old order changeth. I can't help feeling you're a lone voice, Squire." Crawford's voice was crisp.

"By no means. The village is with me."

The Squire spoke with conviction and Dan signified his agreement. The tall, stoop-shouldered old man caressed the coat of arms and stared up at the ceiling for a few moments, seeking expression to the thoughts within him.

"You see, Crawford," he said, "this coat of arms doesn't belong to the Lawson-Hopes. It belongs to Ambridge. There are families here that have been here as long as the Manor."

Mine too, thought Cyrus exultantly.

The Squire's thumbs thrust deep into the lower pockets of his waistcoat and he looked at Crawford under his thick eyebrows, kindly and tolerant, yet unable wholly to keep a note of challenge out of his voice.

"There was a Sherman at Sedgemoor with the Lawson-Hopes. There was an Archer in my kinsman's service at Waterloo. A Gabriel was batman to my father at Vimy Ridge. Three dozen men of the village were in the yeomanry regiment of which I was colonel during the last war. We are a community."

"Forgive me," Crawford said gently. "But we're still in the past."

Cyrus suddenly remembered where he had seen him—on an aeroplane over the Atlantic, flying into the dawn. He wanted to break in and claim this new acquaintanceship, but Lawson-Hope was already speaking again.

"It's upon the past that the present and future are built. You're probably a stranger to this sort of—of link, this continuity of purpose we feel inside us. It's the sort of thing to which most of us are incapable of giving articulate expression." He waved his arms in a gesture that embraced the Manor, the village and its history. "Believe me, it means something. The iron-stone scheme will destroy it. If you're prepared to do that then there's nothing more to be said."

Crawford rose and set down his glass.

"I don't think there is much more to be said at the moment." His smile was friendly, but his tone was noncommittal. "I'm glad we had this talk." He held out his hand to the Squire. "I'll be frank. At the moment I'm not convinced by your arguments. But there's no likelihood of Fairbrother and myself putting our names to the dotted line for a week or two, so I've plenty of time to reconsider at my leisure some of the things you've said."

Crawford was preparing to leave when Cyrus, already feeling possessive towards Ambridge, broke in: "You, sir—you know Pittsburg?" When Crawford nodded he went on: "I can see what this gentleman's trying to explain to you. Tradition means a lot to us over there. Think of Pittsburg and maybe you won't be so anxious to tear up this countryside."

"What can this place mean to you—a stranger?" Crawford's curiosity was aroused.

"A link with the past—roots—a sense of belonging." Cyrus peered round at the three men through his glasses. "I love these little old villages. Some Americans would love to transport one, brick for brick and thatch for thatch, all the way back home. Not me. They belong here. So did my ancestors. That's what I've come here for—to see the sort of place they lived in. It pleases me and reassures me to find places haven't changed very much since they were alive——" He remembered the Bull. "Though you could do with some central heating and air conditioning and decent sanitation."

With a perplexed shake of his head Crawford moved towards the door. Dan offered him a lift up to Fairbrother's and Crawford promptly accepted. While he was putting on his coat Dan lingered on the threshold of the library.

"Well, Squire, we tried."

"Without much success, I'm afraid."

"I'll keep at him," Dan said. "Good night, sir. I'll do what I can. Good night, Mr. Standish."

When Lawson-Hope returned from seeing his guests off, he said to the American: "It gives me great pleasure to know we feel the same way about these things."

"Say," said Cyrus eagerly, "perhaps we are related. My mother used to tell me about the Venns from Ambridge. Sounds kind of aristocratic. Are they relations of yours?"

The Squire paused for a moment.

"There aren't any left in the district. They emigrated somewhere or other, I believe. Oh, of course, they went to America. Venn? Venn? Let me think!"

"None with the Cavaliers?" asked Cyrus hopefully.

"No!" The Squire smiled faintly. "The only distant relation you're likely to find is—yes, his mother's aunt married twice—is a man by the name of Gabriel."

"Gabriel!" Cyrus felt deflated and his jaw sagged. "I—er—I've met him."

Trudging down the Manor drive an hour later Cyrus reflected that he would go and do the Shakespeare country after all instead of staying out the rest of his time in Ambridge. The Squire had told him enough about Gabriel to make him content to live with his sentimental dreams rather than face wrinkled reality as personified by Walter.

Yet he was glad he had said what he did to Crawford before he found out about his new relatives. Otherwise, Cyrus thought, his tone might have lacked conviction.

XI

WHEN they left the Manor Dan drove slowly to make the most of his few minutes with Crawford.

"You're all the same, Mr. Crawford, you chaps with the big plans," he rumbled. "We've got 'em in our game, too. Somebody sitting behind a ministry desk somewhere with a load of facts and figures says, 'This is a good scheme. We'll do it.' Doesn't bother to think about the human beings whose lives he's disorganising."

Crawford laughed.

"As a matter of fact I'm beginning to be interesed in human beings, Mr. Archer. That American, for example, was quite pathetic in his interest in tradition."

"Why don't you get around the village a bit and meet a few of us, then?" Dan asked. "You might as well hear all sides of the story before you make up your mind."

"Not a bad idea."

Dan turned into the village street and headed the car in the direction of Fairbrother's.

"This scheme's upset quite a few lives already, I can tell you, Mr. Crawford—and so far it's only been talked about."

"Even I can think of at least one person who's affected," Crawford said.

There was something in his tone that made Dan glance at him, but in the meagre light from the dashboard it was impossible to see the expression on his face.

"I was due to meet your son last night," Crawford went on. "However, I didn't. Grace Fairbrother went out to fetch him in for a drink, but—he didn't come. I noticed that, because she had started to tell me something about the village."

"Oh? Phil said nothing to me." Dan pursed his lips in a soundless whistle, refusing to be drawn by Crawford's remarks.

"Something upset the girl very much. She stayed in her room all day today." Crawford paused. "Ironstone, d'you think?" he asked drily.

Dan brought the car to a halt in front of Fairbrother's house. Crawford expressed his thanks as he got out and was gone.

When Dan got home Doris was getting cocoa and Phil, shoes in hand, was on his way to bed.

"Oi, wait a minute, young feller!"

Phil returned to the kitchen at his father's summons.

"What went on up at Fairbrother's last night, Phil?"

"No idea." Phil shrugged and turned back to the door.

"Wait a minute. What upset Grace?" Dan saw the colour come into Phil's face. "You had something to do with it, whatever it was."

Cup and spoon in hand, Doris looked up, puzzled. "What's been going on, then?" she said.

Phil put on a long-suffering look.

"Jane was tired and went to sleep on a pile of sacks in the office. I went to wake her up and put my arms round her to help her up and at that moment Grace came barging in." He made determinedly for the door again. "She didn't wait for explanations—just hopped it."

His tone was casual, but his face was still flushed.

"And that's all there was to it?" Dan asked.

"It's enough, isn't it? Good-night," Phil snapped.

He closed the door sharply behind him and went whistling with an unconvincing lack of concern down the passage.

"What did happen, Dan?" Doris sounded anxious. "Was that all there was to it—what Phil says?"

"Dunno. But if a comparative stranger like Crawford gets a shrewd idea what was up, it stands to reason Fairbrother did, too."

He sat down and looked soberly at his wife.

"Seems to me young Phil's got to tread pretty carefully or it won't be long before he finds himself looking for another job."

"Grace and Jane, is it?" Doris asked.

"Ay—Grace and Jane. It's coming to a head, by the look of it, and neither of 'em'll be satisfied with the judgment of Solomon. That boy's got to watch his step, or, by George, he'll land himself in a packet of trouble. And the rest of Ambridge with him."

From the gossip he heard around the village in the course of the next day or two, Dan Archer realised that Crawford was following his suggestion of going out and meeting people. The American had disappeared as suddenly as he came, his visit unexplained, but Crawford was still there, talking to people little but listening a great deal.

"Even comes into the Bull for a pint o' nights," Walter Gabriel reported. "Stands his round, too. Mightn't be such a bad feller, y'know, Dan, when you gets to know him."

"He's no fool, Walter," Dan said and made a mental note to look into the pub that evening to see for himself what went on.

By nine o'clock he was puffing contentedly at his pipe and, elbow on the counter, listening to the voices of the men grouped around the blazing fire of old apple logs in the public bar.

Crawford sat on a wooden bench, his back leaning against the plain deal table that time and custom set aside for the exclusive use of crib and dominoes players. His hands were stretched out to the flames and there was a rapt expression on his face. The talk of the three countrymen sharing the fire with him had held his attention for an hour.

Bill Slater, untidy, pugnacious and already a little drunk, walked over to the group with a show of truculent impatience. He held three darts in his hand and made a great show of trying to get into position to throw them. The chairs of two of the men were directly in line with the dartboard, but they did not attempt to move.

"Bill!"

Dan spoke quietly, but his tone was peremptory. The youth looked up and Dan jerked his head in the direction of the door.

"Plenty of room in the other bar if you want to use the dartboard."

Bill opened his mouth to argue, but Dan looked unusually serious and severe. Glowering, Bill picked up his beer and shambled out of the bar.

One of the group at the fireplace raised a finger and Sam, the cheerful landlord, moved about unobtrusively refilling the mugs. When he was back behind the bar he gave Dan a wink.

"They've hooked him, I reckon, Dan," he said softly.

The three men were talking about things Crawford had never seen, or, if he'd seen, failed to recognise, things perhaps only the people of the deep country noticed—the badger doing its spring-cleaning, the faithful guardianship of the male stickleback, the size of a mole's eye, the mad March hares. So vivid and detailed were the pictures they conjured up from their experience that it seemed the quiet bar was peopled with the wild life of the woods, the soft rustlings of dead leaves, the squeaks, the mutterings, the fragments of sound that the practised ear of the naturalist could translate into some exciting episode in the history of a woodland creature.

Tom Forrest, the Squire's gamekeeper, Doris Archer's brother, squat, solid, his leathery features lit up and animated by the story he wove, crouched forward on the edge of his chair, his gaitered legs and heavy boots outspread, his hands gripping an imaginary gun. Attentive, Crawford encouraged him with his eyes, the eyes of a shrewd business man.

"There you are in the reeds at dusk, Mr. Crawford, with the chap next to you fifty yards away and you can't see him," Tom was saying in his rich drawl, his eyes gleaming as he lived again the excitement of the moment. "There you are and the partridges have finished that grating evening hymn of theirs and are settling down in the grass for the night and the little owls are beginning to screech along the hedges."

Walter Gabriel nodded. He was sitting on the bench beside Crawford, thumbs in the armholes of his waistcoat, boots steaming on the fender.

"Main cold it can be, too—cold and wet and miserable this time o' year, but you ain't thinkin' about that—not when the evening flight's coming in to feed."

Crawford's glance went back to Tom Forrest.

"Presently they come." Tom's arm went up. "First it's the snipe—calling away up there, *scape—scape*, zigzagging across the sky. You can hardly see 'em. Then—whoosh! Down they dives with a rush of wings and settles almost afore you can get a shot at 'em."

"Ay, that's right enough." Simon, the wiry little man who had worked for Dan for twenty years, gave a chuckle. "Got to be sharp with snipe, you have."

He leant forward, took a poker from the fire and plunged it, sizzling, into his mug of cider, watching the steaming froth cream out.

"After them comes the teal." He took the poker out and swung it like a gun. "You can hear 'em—a sharpish double whistle like a rusty door-hinge—but they're proper devils to see. They fly in fast and low and I reckon if one perched on your muzzle there's times you wouldn't know it."

The three men of Ambridge nodded to themselves, remembering teal hit and teal missed. Crawford's expression had mellowed and was one of mingled envy and regret that he, too, had not shared their experiences.

Bill Slater calling loudly for beer at the hatchway to the other bar did nothing to distract Crawford's attention.

Turning, Dan looked in level disapproval at young Bill, framed in the serving hatch. Wayward, stubborn, the youth met his glance for a few seconds, then with a mutter turned away and threw his darts fiercely at the board.

Young fool, Dan thought. He'll be in serious trouble if he doesn't pull his socks up. What's got into him? Not so very long ago he was a pleasant enough fellow, trying to adapt himself to his environment. He would never lose his accent or that street-corner slouch which looked so out of place around a farm, but at least he had been harmless.

Recently, though, something unwholesome and resentful seemed to have become part of his character. He was rude, lazy, rebellious. According to Doris, he was not ill—whatever was wrong with him was a malaise of the spirit, she said. It didn't alter the fact that he was becoming harder to handle. Dan had been galled to the point where he had been ready to dismiss Bill. But that would have been like kicking a sick dog. Besides, because he was related to young Jack's wife, Dan felt a personal responsibility towards the lad.

Dan's glance returned to the fireplace. The pattern of wrinkles around Walter Gabriel's eyes became more intricate as he squinted up to the ceiling.

"Mallard follows the teal," he was saying. "Flyin' fairly high, wings whistlin' and the drakes callin' *gug-gug-gug* all excited like as they spots the feeding grounds."

One hand went to Crawford's shoulder, the other traced the imaginary flight of the birds.

"Round they swings and down they comes, droppin' in with their paddles forward and their heads stretched out and the air whistlin' through their wings . . ." Walter watched the birds down, took a long pull at his beer and heaved a satisfied sigh. "Wonderful sight— wonderful."

Crawford turned, caught Dan's eye, and they smiled together. He stood up, stretched, and waved at his three companions.

"Fill 'em up, landlord. This round's on me." Turning to Tom Forrest, he said politely, almost sadly, "Thanks for telling me all the things I've missed in my life."

"We shall miss 'em too, sir," Tom said ponderously and, seeing the bewildered look on Crawford's face, got around to the point the three of them had been trying to make all evening.

"Funny things, wild creatures, y'know, Mr. Crawford. Take them birds we've been talking about. They mightn't come back to Ambridge again if they took a dislike to something like ironstone workings, for instance."

"That's quite a thought," said Crawford non-committally.

Dan, watching, imagined that his expression had softened.

Desultory conversation filled the bar. Mugs were replenished and Crawford was reaching in his pocket for his money when Fairbrother came in.

Talk died immediately. Dan filled the embarrassing hush by offering him a drink.

"No thanks, Mr. Archer." Fairbrother was cool and rather hurried. "I saw your car outside, Crawford. I wondered if you'd care to give me a lift back to the farm."

"Delighted. You're in no hurry, I suppose?"

"Well . . ." Fairbrother looked at his watch.

"You see, this happens to be my round," Crawford explained. "You'd better have one."

"No, I won't, thanks," said Fairbrother brusquely.

Covertly Dan studied Fairbrother, standing ill at ease midway between the bar and the door. Fairbrother was watching Crawford closely, noting his companionship with the men around him. A slight lift of his eyebrows betrayed his surprise when he heard Crawford calling them by their Christian names.

He's worried, Dan thought. Wants to get him away before they can work on him too successfully.

Fairbrother fidgeted with his gloves.

"I—I——" He cleared his throat. "I think I'll wait in the car, Crawford."

"Eh?" Crawford looked up. "All right, old boy. I won't be a moment or two."

Hurrying him along, Dan thought.

The bar door burst open and Fairbrother's path was blocked by Bill Slater. The youth swayed slightly on his feet. His face had the sour expression of a man who had no friends and gloried in his unhappy solitude.

"What's the matter, then? Too high and mighty for the spit and sawdust?" His voice was insolent. "Isn't the company good enough for you? Not enough brass, eh?"

Fairbrother compressed his mouth and tried to brush past, but Bill edged quickly in front of him. The men at the bar turned disapprovingly.

"That'll do, Bill!" Dan's voice was sharp.

Slater ignored him. He moved forward a couple of paces unsteadily, and held Fairbrother's lapels.

"You bust Ambridge wide open with your ironstone and I'll bust you, see?"

Fairbrother's eyes narrowed and his jaw hardened. His hands fastened around Bill's wrists and slowly, firmly, forced his arms down. Bill crouched, bunching his muscles ready for a fight, his unkempt hair falling over his eyes and his mouth twisting.

"Get him, somebody," old Sam rapped. "None o' that in here."

Dan and Simon moved quickly. Before Bill could throw a punch they slipped between him and Fairbrother and bundled the youth out of the door.

Dan shoved him roughly into a chair in the passage. "Watch him, Simon. The young fool's been spoiling for a fight all evening." He turned to see Crawford buttoning his overcoat and Fairbrother watching him grimly. "Sorry about that, Mr. Fairbrother."

Fairbrother gave a curt nod of acknowledgment and led the way out of the door. Crawford followed, hands plunged deep in his overcoat pockets and shoulders hunched.

Standing over Bill's chair, Tom Forrest voiced the thoughts running through Dan's mind in a scathing, contemptuous tone.

"Couldn't have done it better if you'd wanted the scheme to go through, you whelp. We were getting on well with Crawford, but what d'you think he thought of that exhibition o' yours, eh?"

"Wrong-headed as all the sabotage that's been going on up at Fairbrother's," Walter rasped. "Doesn't do our case any good at all. You're a fool, Bill Slater—a drunken young fool."

Bill sat with his hands hanging loosely between his knees, stubborn and unrepentant, interjecting grunts and curses while the men told him what they thought of him.

Ten minutes later Christine came in, her round fair face flushed. She seemed irritated.

"I've just run into Mrs. Perkins, Bill. She wondered where you'd got to and was coming to look for you. She's had your tea in and out of the oven for the past two hours."

Walter reached down and pulled the youth to his feet.

"Get off home with you," he said, fingering the buckle of his heavy belt. "Off out of it 'fore I gives you a damn good latherin'!"

"What's been happening?" Christine asked when the door closed on him.

She frowned as they told her.

"What a daft thing to do. I've no patience with Bill Slater. I wasn't long, was I, Dad?"

"Meeting over?" he asked. She had been to a cricket-club dance committee meeting, helping to arrange the annual winter dance that raised funds for new kit every summer.

"Not quite—I slipped away early."

When Dan and Christine left they did not see Bill Slater in the darkness lounging against the old stone mounting block outside the Bull, although they passed within a yard of him. He watched their progress across the narrow car park and a vindictive expression twisted his emaciated face when a burst of laughter from Christine came back to him through the night.

A few hundred yards down the village street the cricket-club dance committee meeting was breaking up. A single electric-light bulb shone in the drab junior schoolroom with its depressing brown paint and yellow distemper, relieved only by the gaily coloured travel posters and paper cut-outs pinned around the walls.

A group of half a dozen people stretched with relief after squatting in the undersized desks. One or two gave their hands a last warm on the radiator before going out, while the tidy-minded brushed flattened cigarette ends into a neat pile on the wooden floor.

The secretary folded up his papers and put his minute book away in his briefcase. He picked up a bunch of keys and stood looking at his watch.

"What about these keys?" He lived at the other

end of the village and liked to have a drink or two before he went home.

"Leave 'em," Phil Archer volunteered. "I'll lock up and drop 'em in on the caretaker."

A minute or two later only Phil and Jane remained in the schoolroom, taking a last look round to make sure the place had been left reasonably tidy.

"Does the cricket club always have its dance just after Christmas?" Jane asked.

"One of 'em. If it's a success, we have another." Phil was trying to fish a cigarette butt out of an inkwell with a pen nib. "Why?"

"Oh . . . nothing."

But she seemed restless.

"Were you wondering whether we might still be here, Jane? Up at Fairbrother's, I mean?"

"Sort of."

His thoughts went back to the night a week ago when he'd held her in his arms—the disastrous night when Grace surprised them by coming into the farm office.

Since then everything had been unsettled. He had not seen Grace since and wondered if she were purposely avoiding him. He and Jane had not referred to the incident but behaved as though it had never happened. Phil felt he did not know where he stood; he sensed that his position at the Fairbrother farm was precarious. And over everything was the threat of ironstone.

"Did you realise I was thinking of packing it in?" he asked.

"I could see." Jane toyed with the bunch of keys on the desk. "Chris told me tonight that there's going to be a public enquiry. And I got the impression from her you didn't care any more whether the scheme goes through or not."

Phil gave up the struggle of trying to get the sodden mess of tobacco out of the inkwell, returned the pen to its tray and moved over to the girl. She was wearing a simple black frock with a string of pearls at her throat. It was a contrast to her tweeds and careless workaday appearance. Tonight Phil saw her as strangely and excitingly feminine.

"Jane—if I made up my mind to leave Fairbrother's, what would you do?"

Her interest seemed centred on the bunch of keys.

"I think I'd like to come with you and get a job with you—wherever you go."

"Why?"

The pale light of the bare electric bulb shining down on her smooth forehead gave an added lustre to the casual disarray of her auburn hair, highlighted against the background of the school blackboard.

She looked at him and smiled—a smile that seemed to be able to find amusement in the fact that he should ask the question.

"Because I think you're wonderful," she said, with that tantalising, half-mocking, half-encouraging, wholly feminine tone which he had always considered characteristic of Jane.

He moved a step nearer to her.

"Do you really think so?" he asked, flattered, pleased, still wondering. Looking down, he could see the light reflecting from the sheen of her auburn hair. He could see the downcast dark lashes and her smiling curved mouth. She was wearing a provocative scent that made him long to draw her into his arms. But, remembering the last time, he hesitated.

"As if I'd tell you," she teased. Then she linked her arm in his and they walked out companionably together. Enchantment had brushed them for a moment, then had left them—friends.

But in the dark, when she came closer to him for warmth and rubbed her soft forehead against his chin, the old affection blazed, and he took her into his arms with a tender regard that banished all memories of any girl but Jane.

XII

NEXT morning Walter Gabriel reported everything to Dan Archer as he had seen it through his mischievous old eyes.

"Kissin' and cuddlin', they was, Dan."

Gaze concentrated on the hedge twenty yards in front of him, Walter stepped sideways over the frost-hardened grass a few paces nearer his neighbour. "It's a fact. Saw 'em sparkin' wi' me own eyes. Behavin' like a real courtin' couple. Down by the school, it was. Last night."

"Very likely." Dan nodded.

"Grace ain't goin' to like that." Walter chuckled. "Jane liked it, though. Reckon 'er was as interested in a cuddle as young Phil was. I saw 'em, Dan."

The dusky shape of a rabbit appeared from the burrow, paused for a split second, then darted down another hole a yard away. Hard on its heels a pink-eyed, sleek, creamy-yellow form showed up for a moment against the black tracery of the winter hedge-row, moving among the tangled roots with the sinuous grace of a snake. The ferret disappeared underground again and the three watching men quietly eased their positions. Gun muzzles lifted an inch or two in anticipation. Cold fingers, lying straight along trigger guards, were flexed ready to fire.

A minute passed in silence except for the scratching of another ferret in the carrying box at Dan's feet, restive at the scent of the dozen dead rabbits legged and hanging from the handle of the spade nearby.

A rabbit bolted from the menace of the ferret in the burrow. At the other side of the hedge Tom Forrest already had his gun to his shoulder. There was a sharp crack and the rabbit dropped in its tracks, ten yards from the hole from which it had emerged.

"There's more in there yet," Dan said, thumbing his safety catch.

"Reckon he'll marry her?" Walter persisted.

"I wish you'd shut up," Dan grunted. "Pay attention to your shooting, you old gossip."

"I just been thinkin', that's all, wonderin' if Phil and Jane'll make a do of it. They're goin' the right way about it from what I've seen." Walter chuckled again. "That'll put Phil in queer street up at Fairbrother's, I reckon, jiltin' the gaffer's daughter like that——"

Somewhere underground a rabbit shrieked.

"Dang it, he's killing." Walter disgustedly lowered the hammers of his ancient gun. "I'll get the liner."

Tom Forrest was flat on his stomach at one of the holes, listening.

"Let Lass try, Tom." Dan flicked his fingers and the collie that was patiently sitting behind him sprang up, tail wagging. "Find him, then. Find him. Good bitch."

Nose down, Lass moved from hole to hole until, barking, she caught the scent, rammed herself hard into the burrow and, finding it too small, backed out and tore at the earth with her paws.

"She knows it's there, Tom," Walter said. He took the other ferret from its box, snapped a line on to its collar and brought it to the hole. "Out the road, Lass, or you'll get your nose nipped."

Tom put the ferret down the hole and paid out the line as it travelled through the burrow. The main use of the line was to make the ferret easier to locate after the kill.

"Just like old Dan," Walter grumbled. "Allus the same. When we're all ready to pack he says, ' We'll just put 'im down once more.' And what happens? The blessed thing kills and lies in there and we wastes an hour diggin' to get 'im back."

Dan fished for his pipe.

"We haven't done so bad for a couple of hours," he said. "Thirteen isn't bad. And we know there's at least one more down there."

Presently the worker ferret, driven off from the kill by its stronger companion on the line, appeared at the mouth of one of the holes. Chirruping to it through his pursed lips, Dan picked it up and returned it to its box.

"How would you like young Jane for a niece?" Walter asked Tom, shaking the rabbits from the shaft of the spade. "'Cos it looks as though you're a-goin' to get her."

"That right, Dan?" Tom gave the line a tentative jerk and, squatting on his haunches, looked up at his brother-in-law. "It's serious, is it?"

"So Walter says."

Dan watched Tom at work. The slim, curved blade of the spade in his hands—the "grafter" they called it— bit down into the soil as the gamekeeper hurled his weight on it. Tom had a reputation of being almost clairvoyant when it came to pinpointing the spot under which he judged rabbit and ferret should lie. And once the grafter was in his hands he attacked the ground in a great hurry, whether it was easily dug soil or stones and knotted roots. Walter and Dan looked at each other knowingly. Tom was working up a sweat; he was thoroughly happy.

"From what I hear of it," Tom said in between thuds of the grafter on the soil, "Jane'll be a good capture for any young farming man."

"She ain't no ugly duckling, neither." Walter slipped his penknife back in his pocket after legging the rabbit Tom had shot a few minutes earlier. "'Tain't just hanky-panky 'tween her and Phil. You can see by the way they behave."

Dan nodded. He'd noticed that in the last fortnight Jane had changed subtly. There were times when she looked radiantly happy. Perhaps she *was* in love.

He wasn't so sure about Phil. True he was always ready with a smile for Jane—the sort of smile that might indicate shared secrets and confidences—but at other times he seemed uneasy and restless, unsure of himself.

"I reckon the ironstone business has upset the apple-cart for quite a few folk," Dan said. "Fairbrother and Grace have just about put themselves beyond the pale. Wish the stuff had never been found."

He looked across the rolling countryside and mentally plotted the limits of the ironstone field, imagining it ravaged by the ugliness of an opencast mine.

"Well, I suppose the next day or two'll tell," he said. "It all rests on what happens at the public enquiry. I see by the *Borchester Echo* that one has been called after all. Suppose the reporters will turn up at that— maybe they'll be on our side."

"I'm on him!" exclaimed Tom triumphantly. He dropped the grafter and, reaching down, pulled the ferret from the neat hole he'd dug down to the burrow. "Here, Walter. Take the liner."

Like a magician producing rabbits from a hat, he flipped out the animal the ferret had killed, hauled out three more live rabbits from the hole and despatched them with a deft blow behind the head.

"That's the lot."

"Good. Milking time now," Dan said.

The three men packed up and made their way across Fairbrother's fields back towards Brookfield.

"Crawford's gone up to London, hasn't he?" Tom asked in his flat drawl. "Think he'll be down again for the public enquiry?"

"Can't say," Walter replied. "Folks say he ain't signed over the mineral rights of the Manor estate to Fairbrother yet, though."

At the gate of Dan's orchard they halted at the sound of a hunting horn and hounds in the distance.

"Didn't expect 'em this way," Tom said. "The meet was at Hollerton crossroads."

"They're a-comin', anyway!" Walter dropped his load and clambered up into the hedgerow to get a better view. "Dog fox as they've picked up far from home, more than likely—one that's given 'em a long, straight run."

The pack came streaming into view, followed by the leaders of the field in full gallop. In the next field Dan's old carthorse, Blossom, pricked up her ears, snorted and trotted heavy-hoofed up and down the hedge.

"Look at the old fool getting excited," Dan laughed. "Holding her head up and tossing her mane as though there was a time when she used to lead the field herself."

Two fields away the pack turned and bore away towards the woods. Half a dozen riders put their mounts at the hedge with varying success. One or two went over clean, others left gaps and broken branches to mark their passage. There was excitement in the air and the thrill of the chase in the music of the horn, the thudding hooves and short, snorted breaths of the hard-ridden horses.

The heavy old carthorse gave a wild whinny, racing at a lumbering gallop up and down the hedge. Clods of earth flew up from her broad hooves as they dug into the turf.

"Be blowed if she don't think she's as good as they are!" Walter grinned.

Tail and neck arched high, Blossom slithered to a halt and, stamping and snorting, backed up a little. Dan's amused expression suddenly changed to one of concern. The horse was suddenly pathetic, like a fat heavy old woman envying the grace and agility of a girl.

"The blame thing's going to try and jump!" He dropped his gun and started to run, yelling at the bemused carthorse. "Whoa, Blossom! Whoa!"

Blossom went straight for the five-barred gate—a short, almost prancing charge of a few paces. The huge, barrel-like body rose ambitiously, but she could not lift her hindquarters. The heavy belly descended on the top bar of the gate. It gave under her weight and snapped with a noise like a pistol shot. Blossom hung half-over, hooves kicking the lower bars and scrambling ineffectually in the dirt.

"Whoa, now! Whoa!" Dan scrambled over and grabbed the blowing horse's forelock. "You're hung up. There's a blessed pickle to put yourself in!"

The horse quietened down and the three men made a quick examination. It was impossible to move Blossom forwards or backwards. High spirits and dreams of attainment gone, the animal hung its head and, blowing hard, waited for them to do something.

"Dan, me old beauty," Walter said gravely, "looks to me as though you've gone and lost yerself a damn fine gate."

"Yes—nothing else for it, I'm afraid," Dan sighed.

He went up to the house, warned Simon and Bill that they would have to do the milking themselves and fetched a saw. The light was already failing when he got back to the horse, and it took another hour to saw through the gate and set her free.

"Better take her up to the stables for a day or two to keep an eye on her," Tom advised.

"I'll give the old fool some bran mash, although she doesn't deserve it."

Christine, Phil and Doris had already had their tea by the time Dan got into the house. Doris had been down to the village during the afternoon and was full of news of preparations for the public enquiry. For a while, Ambridge had thought that Lawson-Hope and his lawyers might be able to settle the dispute without a public enquiry being needed, but feeling had become so high that only an impartial outsider would be able to get to the core of truth in the dispute.

Doris was saying, "The village hall's all ready—laid out like a court. There's a table with a navy blue blanket on it for the man who's conducting the enquiry —pink blotting paper, pens, pencils and a carafe of water. Counsel for Mr. Fairbrother's staying at the Bull. The Squire's and the farmers' lawyer is having dinner at the Manor tonight."

She took a deep breath.

"Then there's all the clerks and hangers-on and heaven knows who else putting up at the Bull, and all the farmers are meeting up at Squire's after dinner and Phil says somebody got into Fairbrother's barn last night and ripped two dozen sacks of corn and let it all out over the floor——"

Dan raised his eyebrows and Phil nodded in confirmation.

"Sabotage again," he said, but Doris was still talking.

"And that nice dark young fellow, Dick Raymond, is going to report on the whole enquiry for the *Echo*, and the poor boy's worried about doing all the writing in time so I told Christine to go down and say he could have his meals here with us in spite of the fact that we hardly know him, and—oh dear, I'm talking rather a lot, aren't I?"

Doris was not alone. There was much talk in the village that evening centred around the public enquiry. Every stranger, every bulky briefcase was reported upon and considered. Uneasy speculations could be heard on every side. There were rumours that Fairbrother was so confident of success that he had already ordered mining equipment, wilder rumours that the Ministry of Agriculture had intervened. Almost everyone had a personal interest, but the outcome could not be forecast.

Ambridge spent a restless night.

XIII

WHEN the public enquiry opened in the village hall the next morning Grace Fairbrother drove down from the farm with her father and quietly took a seat while he exchanged a few words with his barrister.

She thought her father was showing signs of strain and she knew her own face was pale and drawn. She wished she could explain that the gulf separating the two of them from the rest of the village was not of her own making.

She craned round, searching for some small indication of friendliness and sympathy in the faces around her. Only the Squire gave her a curt formal nod.

But somewhere behind her a voice said, "Supercilious minx."

Too numbed to be hurt, she turned back and stared blankly at the stage. The enmity of these people would not matter so much, she thought, if only she could be sure of Phil. All he'd said when they left the farm that morning was, "This is the big day, isn't it?" and Grace and her father had driven away, leaving Phil and Jane alone together in the office. . . .

"Our counsel is very confident, Grace." She realised that her father had joined her. "We have plenty of expert evidence to support us."

She nodded, unable to speak.

It soon became apparent that the legal representatives of both parties intended to employ no advocates' tricks. They relied on the presentation of facts.

On one hand there was talk of the food that would be lost if the scheme went through: so many tons of bacon and butter . . . so much bread and meat . . . so much milk . . . enough to feed so many thousands for so many years. On the other hand, it was market prices of foreign ores . . . increased shipping charges . . . how much steel the ironstone field would yield . . . what the steel could produce in equipment and machinery.

"Guns or butter," Grace thought. It was the old, old argument of whether peace was best served by optimism or by defence.

Sitting near her, as close to the front as they could get, were an old couple. They craned forward intently, hands cupped to their ears, brows furrowed anxiously. She knew they were old-age pensioners, who would lose their cottage if the scheme went through.

"What's he saying, Fred?" she heard the old lady whisper. "Anything about us?"

It was obvious they heard little and understood even less. Grace knew the old man was born in that cottage and had lived there all his life.

"Wouldn't never leave 'ere for all the tea in China, Miss Grace," he had once told her.

He wanted to spend the rest of his days there, to die and be buried from there. His needs were meagre and his world small. He wanted to keep the only home he had ever known. How his simple wishes were related to the cost of a shipload of iron ore was beyond his comprehension.

Grace leaned over and spoke quietly to her father.

"All accounted for," he returned casually. "They'll be found alternative accommodation——"

"But it's their home——"

"Ramshackle and dilapidated. Should have been

144

condemned years ago. Pump in the yard. Earth closet. No need to get sentimental over it."

She hunched herself deeper into her chair.

"I mustn't think," she told herself. "I must pretend everything's all right. I mustn't remember what this is doing to people—what it's doing to me, to Daddy, to Phil. If I do, I'll go mad and scream the place down."

Before the lunch adjournment the Town Planning inspector who was conducting the enquiry announced he wished to re-examine the land involved in the scheme. He would be ready to hear further evidence at three o'clock.

The day wore on. Witnesses came and went, the evidence piled up, the lawyers argued. All Grace could think about was her own misery and loneliness.

"I can't stay here any longer," she whispered to her father. "If I do I'll go crazy."

"Eh?" He looked puzzled. "But it's going so well, Grace! There's nothing to worry about. Relax."

As she came out of the village hall she felt completely defenceless. She knew there would be eyes watching her all the way up the street. From behind lace curtains, from behind hedges, hostile glances would note the drawn lines of her face. There would be sniggers and morsels of gossip. People were pleased because Jane was taking Phil away from her—Jane who had some-how become the champion of Ambridge because she was depriving Fairbrother's daughter of what she most needed—Phil's love.

She could not face the walk up the street but turned in at the public path by the football pitch and went across the fields. There were fresh molehills where the little creatures had dug deep to avoid the colder weather. A pike lurking in the chill grey waters of the trout stream glided away as she stepped on the little footbridge. But she had no eyes for the things going on around her.

Grace could not quell her suspicions. Jealousy of the girl who had become her rival urged her to approach the farm office quietly. Once before she had surprised them.

Half afraid of what she might see, she glanced in through the open door of the farm office.

Only Jane was there, quiet, methodical, efficient, sorting out different-coloured poultry rings from a box.

"Hullo, Grace." She sounded calm, sure of herself. "High jinks all over?"

Grace shook her head.

"I came away, that's all." She wanted to know where Phil was, how long it was since Jane was with him, what they'd been doing all day, but she dared not ask. "Why don't you go down?"

Jane strung some poultry rings on a piece of binder twine and hung them on a nail.

"Tomorrow." She turned and her tawny eyes looked steadily into Grace's. "Phil said we'd find a spare hour to go down some time tomorrow." Her casual use of "we" was like a blow in the face.

A gleaming yellow plastic poultry ring slipped on to the third finger of Jane's left hand, probably by design. She laughed and held her hand out for Grace to see. "Pretty, isn't it?"

Grace turned on her heel and left the office.

In the privacy of her own room she lay on the bed and sobbed for an hour, humiliated by her helplessness, angry to find she was so weak that a taunt from Jane could hurt her so much.

If there had been someone to whom she could talk— her mother, or a friend of the type like Christine, though not Christine herself—her misery might have been easier to bear. But there was no one to whom she could confide her irrational but overpowering love for a man who did not seem to care.

She heard her father return. Sounds from the kitchen told her that the cook was preparing dinner and she thought that perhaps her father had brought back his legal advisers. She spent a long time putting on fresh make-up, steeling herself to go down and meet them. Her dressing-table mirror told her she was wasting her time. Her pallor showed through the rouge, her eyes were red-rimmed. No cosmetic had been invented that could conceal the saddened droop of her mouth or the blurred contours of her eyes.

Downstairs she sighed with relief to find her father alone. He was getting a whisky and soda from the sideboard.

"You should have stayed with us, Grace." He took his drink with relish and she could sense the air of confidence and good spirits in him—"bouncy" her mother had once called it. "My chap really gave 'em socks later on. It's going very well—for us."

"Is it?"

"By jove, I wish Crawford had been here. If he had any doubts about this scheme he'd be thoroughly convinced after hearing the evidence put up today."

Her vision swam. She stood in the centre of the room crying silently.

"Matter of fact I'm having a transcript of the evidence sent to his London office," Fairbrother went on. "It's high time he signed on the dotted line. Then we'll get a good mining contractor in and——"

He stopped in mid-sentence when he turned from the fire and took his first real look at Grace.

"What on earth——"

She shook her head, unable to speak for the tightness of her throat.

"Grace!"

He stepped forward and his arms went round her shoulders, but she pushed him away.

"Go away—go away!"

Sinking into an armchair, she abandoned her control and wept. Sobs shook her.

"Grace, my dear." Her father's voice was strained. He put an ineffectual hand on her arm, but she turned her back and hid her face in a cushion.

"I've tried to tell you, Daddy. I've tried to warn you. I've tried to keep faith with you. You're asking too much. The sacrifice is too great."

"I don't understand——"

"How could you understand? You can't feel any more. You can't see you're destroying everything that's important to people . . . to me. You've got ironstone in your soul!"

George Fairbrother was so shocked at her accusation that he could hardly answer her.

"Grace, I—I just don't understand." He leant over her armchair and tried to pull her up, but she remained with her face turned into the cushion. "Why are you so unhappy?"

"You don't care about people any more. What happens to anyone doesn't matter, so long as you can push your beastly ironstone scheme through."

Her vehemence puzzled him. It was unlike her to feel so deeply over broad issues. There was more behind her unhappiness than that.

"Grace—how have I hurt you?" He could accept the fact that she was sufficiently illogical to side with the Ambridge people, but why was she taking the matter so personally? "Tell me what's wrong."

"Everything."

He smiled to himself. So it was "everything" again. He knew what to do.

His memory flew back over the years: Grace as a toddler in tears over an ice-cream dropped in the mud; Grace pouting in her first gym slip and those crimson ribbons that set off her two raven plaits so well; her first grown-up party and the disappointment of finding there was no special thrill in staying up after ten at night. . . .

"Everything!" He'd heard it so often before. He admitted to himself that he had rather spoiled her.

When she was small and in one of her hurt moods, he used to open his jacket for her to snuggle her head inside like a kitten, and gradually, as she became quiescent, he would get to the truth. "Everything" was whittled down to some specific fact. . . .

He persuaded her to come and sit beside him on the settee and soon he felt the movement of her head against his chest. Her sobs quietened as he put his arm around her.

"Why are you doing this?" she asked.

"I don't know." Perhaps it was because of his memories, he thought. Perhaps because she seemed so small, so frail and childlike a few moments ago when she was crying in the armchair. "I always used to."

"Not for a long time."

"No, perhaps not."

"Not since I was about fourteen, before Mother died."

He said nothing but pulled his coat more closely around her and comforted her with his arms.

"I'm not a child any more, Daddy."

His fingers moved over her brow, smoothing back wisps of hair from her half-closed eyes. He did not attempt to talk but gazed into the fire, waiting patiently. From experience he knew she could not be hurried. Some minutes passed before she spoke again.

"People have changed since this ironstone business started." He could feel her body trembling. "You've changed. Because you met opposition you've dug your heels in and now you're fighting. And you'll go on till you've had your way."

"Only because I believe the scheme can't bring anything but good to the district," he said reasonably. "It's not just a bee in my bonnet. There must be something in it or it could never have got as far as a public enquiry."

"But you can't be blind to how it's changing people——"

"Who, for instance?" he asked.

He had to wait a few moments for her whispered answer.

"Phil."

"Philip?" They were getting to the roots of the matter at last. "How has he altered?"

"He—he doesn't care about me any more. There—there's ironstone between us."

"Has he said so?"

"No, but I know."

"Come now. People don't alter just like that."

"He has. We're not the same any more. We've drifted for months."

"And you really believe it's because of the scheme?"

"Yes. He's got Jane now. He doesn't want me."

Surprised at his own ignorance, Fairbrother discovered the scheme had occupied so much of his mind that what he noticed around him failed to register properly. Now that he thought about it, he could recall the number of times he had seen Phil and Jane together. He ruefully remembered thinking, some weeks back, that it was good to see manager and poultry girl working so well in harmony.

"What d'you want me to do, Grace—sack him?"

She looked shocked.

"Oh no!"

"Sack her, then?" he asked, as a logical alternative.

"It wouldn't do any good." She shook her head. "It's too late now to do anything. I've lost him."

He looked down at her and said quietly: "It's never too late. Moreover, I think you're putting too much blame on the scheme."

"That started it. Phil has never played around before—not since I met him, anyway."

"Maybe, but I don't think taking sides over the scheme can alter real affections. Isn't it likely that Philip may have grown fond of Jane in any case, scheme or no scheme?"

"I suppose so." She extricated herself from his jacket and sat up, tidying her hair.

"Grace—if I could sincerely and honestly believe that the scheme's to blame I'd throw it in tomorrow, you know that. But it isn't the scheme that's your rival —it's Jane. It's simply one girl against another—and you've had the better start. Admit to yourself that you are partly to blame, and your battle is half won."

She smiled and said, "I'm sorry you've fathered a hysteric," and he knew she was regaining her composure.

He returned to a subject he had mentioned earlier. "I can easily sack her and send her packing if you want her out of the way."

"No." Grace was firm. "I wouldn't want that." Her chin came up determinedly. "You aren't the only one who can be a fighter. We neither of us take the easy way out."

XIV

THE YOUNG reporter from the *Borchester Echo* was weary. By mid-afternoon on the second day of the public enquiry he felt his arm was ready to drop off. The sheer physical strain of taking down in shorthand the thousands of words that had been spoken since the enquiry opened was telling on him.

Dick Raymond had been in and out of Ambridge many times during the past few months. In his work he had passed beyond the stage of making tea and carrying copy around the newspaper office. He had passed the stage where, full of self-importance, he had ridden a rusty bicycle through Borchester, meeting trains and buses to see if any of them carried messages for his paper. In the course of a busy but tiring time as a proof reader, he had found his dreams of success in Fleet Street becoming a little tarnished. Then they became clear again when he was given a motor-bike and a district which included Ambridge. Everything that happened within the district was his concern. He was supposed to get to know all the people and the local politics.

Occasionally he felt a little scornful about wasting his time, but in his heart he knew that his training was very valuable as a solid basis for more spectacular success elsewhere. Dick had a good memory for names and faces, and a quick sympathy which made him keep the confidence of the people he had to interview. Though sometimes he pretended to be tough and lackadaisical, he had a zeal for his profession and a passionate affection for his paper which had already marked him as a man who would go far.

A legal wrangle between two barristers over proving the accuracy of certain maps that were being put in—interesting, perhaps, to Lincoln's Inn but not to the readers of the *Borchester Echo*—gave him the break he needed. He put down his pencil, massaged his cramped hand and let his gaze travel around the packed village hall, seeking out Christine Archer, whom he knew slightly.

A couple of hours earlier, when he had lunched at Brookfield, she had told him she would be at the enquiry that afternoon.

"I think it's the sort of thing one should go to—to see how democracy works," she had said.

Someone—it was either Phil or his mother—had commented during lunch on how tired and strained Dick looked.

"Must be quite a responsibility," Dan had said. "I know I wouldn't like the job of reporting all that evidence and getting it right."

"It's a fag," Dick had admitted. "But all in the day's work."

"It'll be read, though," Doris had consoled him as she ladled Irish stew and four potatoes on to his plate. "Every word."

Dick had sat up till midnight writing up the first day's proceedings and had been given four and a half columns. In the three years he had been reporting, he had never had quite so much space.

At last he saw Christine, sitting half a dozen rows from the front. She smiled in response to his quick wink —a smile that broadened when his lips soundlessly framed the word "democracy". Then the legal point was settled and he had to pick up his pencil again.

Another witness. Another thousand words verbatim that he'd have to cut down to a hundred if the *Echo* was not to be filled entirely with public enquiry. Another short break and a chance to flex his fingers. . . .

He noticed Phil and Jane come in together and take a seat at the back of the hall. Unconsciously his glance flicked to Grace Fairbrother, sitting straight-backed beside her father two or three yards from the Press table.

Their eyes met and Dick knew she had seen Phil and Jane. The perception which was part of his reporter's training gave him a glimpse of what the girl was suffering behind her impassive mask. He was sorry for her.

The enquiry claimed his attention again, but part of his mind remained with Grace. An hour later, when the proceedings closed, he was not entirely surprised when she came over to his table. All around, now that the business was over, it seemed that advocates, interested parties and spectators could not get out of the hall quickly enough; but Grace remained, watching him collect up his notebooks and copy paper.

"You must have had a lot of experience of these things, Dick."

"Too much," he smiled. "They're good copy, but they get boring after a time." At all costs he must appear blasé on the surface. Secretly, he was thrilled that his editor had trusted him to handle the enquiry alone.

"But you must be able to form some sort of judgment in the light of your experience. How d'you think Daddy'll come out?"

"Well . . ." His mind went back carefully over the evidence given in the past two days. "I'm pretty certain you've won."

"Really?" Her voice was listless as her fingers dragged a pattern of curves on the table.

"Yes, I think the scheme'll go through and Ambridge'll just have to get used to the idea sooner or later."

She thanked him and was turning away when he reached out to take her arm and detain her.

"Grace—there's still another fight. A more personal one."

She looked at him curiously, but he blundered on, trusting that his brashness would be excused by his sincerity.

"You hear things, in a small place like this. Forgive me for mentioning it. I've got nothing against Jane—not a thing in the world. I think she's a nice kid. If the scheme comes off you'll be outside the pale, and I'd like to see you go in and win. Fight for it."

Her lips parted, but again he anticipated her.

"Yes, I know, I've got an awful cheek. Heaven knows why I should be saying this, but an hour ago it suddenly occurred to me that—whichever way the scheme goes—the one person who's been put out on a limb is you."

He stuffed his notebook into his pocket and started to wind his long yellow scarf around his neck. His saturnine features twisted into a wry grin.

"Slap my face if it'll help."

Grace fiddled with her handbag, seeming to find something of interest in the clasp.

"I suppose I'm table-talk at Brookfield," she said quietly. "That's how you arrived at all your conclusions."

"Not entirely. I'd never thought about it until this

afternoon. Then suddenly everything sort of clicked into place."

"I think I know what you mean." Grace considered a moment before she went on. "I may have been rather stupid in the past, but I had a talk with Daddy last night and—got a different perspective."

She looked up and her serious expression softened. It was the first time he had ever seen the warmth of her smile or looked closely at the fragile delicacy of her features and into the depths of her eyes. He could not understand how Phil had ever been able to spurn such an appealing creature.

"Thank you, Dick. You're very kind. And I like you for taking the trouble to talk to me when I need friends." Then her smile froze. Christine, Jane and Phil were coming across to them.

"Goodbye," Grace whispered, and was gone.

Dick stared after her. The others were around him talking, but it was not until Christine nudged him that he became aware of what they were saying.

"My opinion?" he repeated vaguely.

"Wake up, Dick!"

He pulled himself together.

"I think it's Fairbrother's day," he said. Phil and Jane looked glum and Dick smiled consolingly. "Of course, I'm not the bloke conducting the enquiry. I may be wrong."

"Hope so." Phil turned on his heel and took Jane's arm. "See you at Brookfield for tea, Dick."

The enquiry was the main topic of conversation around the tea-table at Brookfield, Dan Archer plying Dick Raymond with a stream of questions in between mouthfuls of food.

"Leave the boy alone, Dan," Doris said. "He must be fagged out after all that work, and he's still got to phone some of today's stuff through to his office."

"That's all right." Dick smiled and turned to Dan. "Well, according to the experts, Mr. Archer, the ironstone will yield about five thousand tons a week. On their estimate that's forty years' work for sixty men."

"Forty years!" Dan whistled. "We've got to be burdened with 'em that long, have we?"

"If the scheme goes through."

"There's nowhere in the village to house sixty men and their families," Doris said musingly. "I suppose it'll mean building a new housing estate. That'll be more good farming land we won't be able to use."

"Ay—and all the youngsters'll go mining," Dan grumbled. "Won't be able to find a farm worker in the place. We can't afford to pay 'em the wages the iron blokes'll give 'em."

"If they're going to be here forty years I'm packing my job in right now," Phil said flatly. "Sixty blokes each pinching one chicken a month for the pot works out at seven-twenty a year or a loss of a thousand quid——"

The others laughed.

"It's a point, though," Phil insisted.

One eye on the clock, Dick hurried through his tea. The others were still at table when he excused himself to phone his copy through. The telephone at Brookfield was out in the passage. He left the kitchen door open for extra light and picked up the receiver. Immediately he heard tinny, distorted voices coming from it and guessed the lines were crossed. He was about to put down the phone when a phrase caught his attention.

Clapping his hand over the mouthpiece he listened with mounting excitement.

"Sssh!"

The group around the table looked up at his warning. Christine came out into the passage.

"What's the matter?"

"This isn't a party line by any chance, is it?" he whispered.

"No—why?"

He gestured her to be quiet and, phone jammed to his ear, listened attentively. By now the rest of the family were grouped around the door. When Dick put down the phone his dark face was ablaze with suppressed excitement.

"Crossed line. Two characters talking. Arranging to sabotage the diesel engine on the mineralogist's drill rig at Fairbrother's tonight."

"Sabotage again!"

The Archers all talked at once.

"Recognise their voices?" Dan asked.

"No. I don't know many people in Ambridge, anyway."

Phil was at the telephone, talking rapidly to the operator. "Are you sure? . . . Oh, okay." He came back into the room and turned his thumbs down. "They can't trace it."

"Call the police," Christine said.

"Not so blooming likely." Phil reached for his coat. "There's only old George Randall. He couldn't cope on his own."

"What're you going to do, Phil?" Doris asked anxiously. She knew that on occasions Phil could be reckless.

"Ambush 'em. Lie in wait. Catch 'em red-handed. I'll get one or two of my chaps together."

"Count me in," Dick said, eager for a story.

"Go careful," Dan warned. "You might get your heads cracked open."

"Not if we see 'em first." Phil was at the door. "Coming, Dick?"

"As soon as I've phoned through my copy. You go ahead. I'll follow you up."

Five minutes later Phil pulled the farm truck to a halt outside the cottage on the Hollerton road occupied by Benson, one of the most reliable workers on Fairbrother's farm. He was about thirty-five, tall, broad and as hard as nails.

"I'll be there, Mr. Archer," he said as soon as he heard Phil's mission. "Glad of the chance to get my hands on 'em."

"Meet me in the farm office in half an hour," Phil said. "And not a word to anybody—not even our own blokes. I'm not saying they've got anything to do with it, but you can't be too careful."

Benson ran his palm over the knuckles of his other hand.

"Trust me, sir. I won't let you down."

Phil arrived at Fairbrother's to find a few strange cars parked in front of the house. He guessed that his employer was entertaining the legal representatives who had done so well for him at the public enquiry. It was Phil's intention to tell Fairbrother the news, but now he decided against it and went to the farm office to lay his plans.

He knew the lorries and drill were sited in the corner of a ploughfield some way from the farmhouse. The hedges and ditches nearby would give adequate cover for him and his companions and he was satisfied they could cover all approaches.

The saboteurs would probably come across the open fields from the trout stream, he thought. Less chance of them being discovered by that route. He would remember to keep special watch in that direction. They had got away with the drill, but if he had his way that would be their last success.

He was searching around the office for a torch to take along with him when Grace came in. She had changed for dinner into a crisp, white, off-the-shoulder gown that brought out her colouring. He looked at her again, uncertain whether she was wearing more make-up than usual or whether she was blushing.

"Want to hear a bit of news, Grace?"

She shook her head. "It'll only be bad news."

"Bad for somebody," he agreed, his mind on the saboteurs.

"Phil."

Something in the quality of her tone made him give up his rummaging in the desk drawer and turn to face her. Her bare shoulders were braced back and she appeared calm, but a tremor in her voice betrayed her.

"Phil—are you happy?"

"Happy?" He did not understand what she was getting at. "How d'you mean?"

"At the moment life's a mess. I suppose it'll be like that as long as this scheme's hanging over our heads."

He nodded slowly, waiting for her to go on.

"I wonder if there is any happiness in the future—away from this ironstone and everything else," she said. "Don't you?"

"It would be a relief to know."

Her intense gaze did not leave his face, and he looked at her oddly, uncertain what to say. She took his arm in a grip so fierce he could feel her nails biting through the cloth of his jacket.

In any other moment but this, Phil would have realised that she was trying to win back his confidence in her. At any other time he would have responded to her affection. But his mind was busy with thoughts of catching the saboteurs, and he had no time for the subtleties and moods of a lovely and desperate girl.

A step sounded outside. Desperately she searched his face for some comfort, for some sign of recognition and interest.

"Say something!" she whispered appealingly.

Phil's lips moved, but before he could speak Dick Raymond walked into the office.

Grace gathered up the skirt of her gown and fled.

Dick looked back, watching the gleaming whiteness of her dress and bare shoulders until the darkness swallowed her up. Kicking the door to, he came to the stove and warmed his hands.

"Been telling Grace about the sabotage?"

Phil shook his head. Hands deep in pockets and shoulders hunched, he stared blankly at the door through which Grace had disappeared.

Dick eyed him curiously. When Phil had left Brookfield a few minutes earlier to lay plans to catch the saboteurs red-handed he had been alert, active and incisive.

"Well?" Dick waited a few moments for Phil to rouse himself. "What's the plan?"

"Eh?"

"Saboteurs. Remember?" Dick teased. "What's got into you?"

He was excited at the prospect of a fight followed by an exclusive story. Phil might be decent enough to show a little more enterprise and vigour.

"Sorry—miles away." Phil ran his fingers through his fair hair, shaking his head as though to clear his brain.

He felt around in his pockets. Dick passed him a cigarette and noticed Phil's hand tremble as he lit it.

"Trouble is, my brain can't deal with too many things at once," Phil said. "I was working out how to cope with the saboteurs when Grace came in and started talking about . . . something entirely different. Looking utterly ravishing, too. Very confusing."

The door opened and the bulky figure of Benson came in. Phil introduced him.

"One of our tougher workers," he said, fitting his hand round the man's biceps. "Useful for an operation such as tonight's."

They spent the next few minutes discussing their ambush plans. Benson, familiar with the farm, quickly understood, but Dick, who had no clear picture in his mind, delayed them with questions. Dick was immensely excited at the prospect of the coming adventure. It fitted in with films he had seen, and books he had read, of intrepid reporters going out to get their copy at first hand. Phil looked at his watch impatiently.

"You'll see it all when we get there," he said. "It'll be clear then. Let's go."

Jane Maxwell almost bumped into them at the office door. She was still in her working clothes but wore a short trench coat over her wellingtons and dungarees to shelter her from the cold of the night.

"What the devil are you doing here?" Phil's tone was sharp.

"I rang Brookfield to see what you were doing tonight," she said simply. "Christine didn't want to talk at first, but I made her. When I found out what was up I came at once."

"Get off back home," Phil snapped.

"You'd better, miss." Benson gave her an avuncular smile. "It'll be no place for a girl."

"Nonsense. I can take care of myself." Her tone was matter-of-fact and she looked at Phil as though she took it for granted there would be no argument.

"You'll be a liability," he said flatly, but relented at once when he saw her look of disappointment. "Oh, all right, come on—but you'll have to do as you're told."

Puzzled by Phil's brusque manner, she fell into step behind the three men and followed them through the darkness. There was no moon, but the sky was cloudless and the misty greyness of the brittle, frosted fields that hissed and crunched under their footsteps was just discernible in the starlight. Ahead of her she could pick out the silhouette of the men. They moved on in silence under cover of the hedges, pausing as they neared the drilling equipment to listen for sounds of the approaching saboteurs.

"Nobody about yet, Mr. Archer. Plenty of time for us to get in position," Benson muttered.

Phil led the way through a gap in the hedge that had been sealed off with a double strand of barbed wire. Benson followed, nimble for a man of such bulk, but Dick got hung up on the wire.

"Hell," Phil said. "I forgot the torch."

They freed Dick in the darkness, fingers exploring the wire until they found where he was caught on the barbs. A few yards away stood the lorries bulked round the spire-like structure of the drill.

Benson moved off to the shadow of a holly bush in

the hedge running at right angles to the one they had come through. Phil took Dick by the arm and led him to the ditch.

"Better straddle it. Liable to be wet underfoot," he said quietly. "Keep watch to the right. They'll probably come by the five-barred gate over there."

"I get it. All clear now," Dick said.

Phil took up a position a few yards farther along the ditch, bracing himself against a tree stump.

"What about me?" Jane asked.

"You stay right here whatever happens and keep out of trouble," he said shortly.

She made no reply but scrambled down into the ditch beside him and stood ankle deep in the icy, muddied water.

For the second time in a few minutes she felt rebuffed. She sensed that something had happened to Phil. She was within a foot of him but knew that from his point of view she might as well not be there.

He is worried, she told herself. Worried about the saboteurs. Worried about my safety. Maybe I am a liability after all.

"Would you sooner I went home, Phil?" she asked softly.

There was a pause while he roused himself from his thoughts.

"Eh?"

"Nothing. It doesn't matter." Timidly she linked her arm in his, then felt him flex his back against the tree stump. "Phil—what's wrong?"

"Can't see much from here," he said. "I'd better move a bit farther along."

She let him go, listening unhappily to the faint sounds of his body brushing against the hedge. The clammy cold of her feet began to creep all through her. Quietly she eased herself out of the ditch and moved along the rimed grass to Dick Raymond. His hand came out and helped her down. Her feet sank into the mud and she felt the chill of the water swirling round her legs again.

"Hullo, Liability!" It was only a whisper, but there was warmth and friendliness in his greeting. "Thought you were with Phil."

"I was, but I don't think I'm popular."

"He's still in his daze, is he?" Dick said quietly.

Daze, she thought, was hardly the word. More like loss of memory—as though something had ruthlessly, abruptly erased from his mind everything that had passed between them. She'd never met this strangeness in him before and it frightened her.

"Poor old Phil," Dick mused. "Shook him rigid."

"What did?"

He did not answer.

"You know something," she insisted. A sudden flash of intuition brought the words to her lips before she could stop them. "Has Grace been with him?"

"Ss-sh. Quiet a minute," he begged.

"Tell me."

He turned away from her and his whole body was tensed, straining towards the five-barred gate. She could barely catch the jerked sentences he muttered between pauses while he looked and listened.

"Dunno much. . . . She was in the office when I got there."

The mud squelched as she started to scramble out, her one thought to get to Phil and claim him for her own.

"Quiet, you ass!" Dick grabbed her coat.

"I must go to Phil!"

"Not now!"

His arms were round her, bearing her down against the hard, sloping bank of the ditch. The touch of the frosty grass against her cheek shocked her into trying to break free from his hold.

"Keep still, you dope, you'll spoil everything," he whispered. "The blighters are coming!"

As he freed her she heard the unmistakable sound of a heavy boot scraping on the bars of the gate. Carefully, silently, she pulled herself upright. The gate and its securing chain rattled as someone climbed over. Straining her eyes through the dark, she detected the movement of two or three shadowy figures making their way silently towards the drill.

Her heart pounded and something seemed to grip at her chest, making it difficult for her to breathe. She realised she was trembling. Beside her she felt Dick gathering himself for the dash across the open space to tackle the intruders. She had lost sight of them now in the bad light but could hear their soft movements among the lorries—the scrape of canvas and the creak of a tailboard being lowered.

"Get 'em!"

Phil's yell rang out sharply on the frosty air. There was an exclamation from one of the saboteurs, and another called, "Hey up! Beat it!"

Dick bolted from the ditch, and Jane heard Phil and Benson pounding in to converge on the drill. She could see little, but before they made contact a figure broke away from the shadow of the lorries and dashed towards her.

The man swerved at the sight of Dick, but the reporter hurled himself for his legs in a flying tackle. They went down together with a gasping thud, arms and legs threshing. The man rolled clear and squirmed to his feet. Dick lunged again to trap his legs, but he back-heeled viciously and his foot connected with the reporter's shoulder. Dick gave a painful gasp and before he could regain his feet the man was racing for the gap in the hedge.

"Stop!"

Jane plunged recklessly along the ditch to try and cut him off, but the clinging mud hampered her. Her fingers scrabbled wildly for the man's leg and fastened on to him for a moment as he ducked through the wire. A sudden jerk as he yanked his leg free sent her stumbling, splashing on hands and knees into the churning water.

"Keep your head down, Jane!"

She heard a sound of tearing cloth and then Dick was leaping over her and grappling with the man, the wire between them. His feet slipped on the frosty bank and the saboteur broke away again, but before he had covered a dozen yards Dick was over the fence and after him.

Soaked and filthy, Jane stood up. The other intruders seemed to be running off in another direction.

"Stay there, Mr. Archer!" she heard Benson call out. "Stick by the drill in case they double back."

She climbed out of the ditch and ran awkwardly towards the lorries, water squelching and sloshing around in her wellingtons. A figure loomed out of the darkness ahead.

"Who's that?" she gasped.

"Me—Phil." He sounded disgruntled. "Ricked my blasted ankle."

"Let me help you——"

"Let's get some light." He brushed her aside, limped over to the cab of the nearest lorry, reached inside and snapped on the headlights. The light lit up the intervening ground and was diffused by the hedge-row. "Can't see much, but it might help Benson and Dick."

He left her at the lorries to go to the hedge and crane over, anxious to see whether the others had made a capture. Jane kicked off her wellingtons, poured out the ditchwater and wrung out the bottoms of her dungarees as best she could. She shivered. The heat and excitement of the past minute or two were spent and her fears returned. She knew the tremor that ran through her body had little to do with her ducking in the icy ditch. . . .

Phil came limping back, tousled and disappointed, squinting against the dazzle of the headlights. He looked pale in the harsh light. Every line of his features was sharply defined, making him look hollow-cheeked, almost haggard. She made him sit on the lorry running-board, took off his shoe and cradled his hurt foot in her lap, exploring his ankle with gentle fingers.

"By God, I hope they catch 'em," he said. "If they get one he'll soon drop his pals in, too."

He lapsed into silence. In the overspill from the headlights she could just see his slumped, listless form, chin on chest and hands thrust deep into his pockets.

A few minutes passed before she eased his foot into his shoe.

"Better try to get it on again, Phil." Here I am, kneeling at his feet like a slave, she thought. "I don't think it's swelling much."

"It'll be okay, thanks." Phil stirred and looked all around him. "Did I hear 'em coming back?"

Impulsively her arms went round his legs and she rested her head in his lap.

"No—please—don't go, Phil!"

"It's all right. I'll see they don't hurt you."

"It isn't that." On her knees beside him, she reached up, her hands touching the lapels of his coat. "It's you. You're falling in love with Grace. Whatever you feel like, please don't go on with it." Her voice broke. "You can't—you can't."

"Jane——"

"It would be all wrong. You're not for her. Can't you see? It would never work out—never, never."

His hands took her by the shoulders and held her away from him so he could see her face.

"How could you have known that's what I've been thinking about all evening?"

"Never mind." Her tawny eyes were staring wide, and a muddy smear across her brow and cheek heightened the grief in her face. "Call it woman's instinct if you like. You won't fall in love with her, will you?"

The flapping of the lorry canvas, stirred by the wind, ticked off the seconds while he looked at her helplessly.

"You're shivering," he mumbled at last. His hands moved over her coat. "You're cold. You're wet through. Poor little Jane."

"Phil, tell me, please—have you suddenly decided to marry her?"

"I—I don't know . . . I just don't know."

Benson came clambering over the gate, his chest heaving after his exertion, and Phil rose to meet him.

"Lost 'em, Mr. Archer." He sat down on the running-board with a thud and expelled his breath in a long sigh. "My two separated in the water meadows. I singled out one of 'em, but he gave me the slip in Squire's woods."

"Recognise either of 'em?"

"Sorry—no." Benson ran his coat sleeve across his sweating brow. "When you switched the lights on they were already down the slope and in shadow."

"Damn. Any sign of Dick?"

"Ain't seen him."

Phil handed round cigarettes. Benson inhaled deeply and was seized with a fit of coughing. His lungs had been too strained to stand the extra irritation of smoke.

"I clouted one pretty heavy," he said when he recovered. "Not in the face, though, worse luck. Somewhere on the body. If I'd got him in the puss we could have gone round the village tomorrow looking for somebody with a couple of loose teeth."

A few minutes later Dick returned, covered in mud, his thumbs turned down.

"Took a header in the ploughfield over there," he said. "I caught up with the bloke a couple of times, but when I went for six in the ploughfield I winded myself. Couldn't get going properly again." Dick put his arm round Jane and gave her a friendly squeeze. "Plucky girl! You almost had the blighter single-handed."

"Is that right?" Phil turned to her. "You didn't say."

"It wasn't important." She moved away from the beam of the headlights so they could not see her face. Nothing seemed important any more, except the numbing realisation that she was not sure of the man she loved. "I did nothing."

"I don't think they'll come back." Benson got into the cab and switched off the headlights. "But I'll stay here for an hour or two just in case."

"Thanks, Benson." Phil sounded dispirited. "I suppose I'd better go and tell Fairbrother we've messed the job up. Come on, you two."

Back in the farm office, when the lights were switched on, Phil looked more closely at Jane, noting her soaked dungarees and sleeves.

"You'd better get straight off to the Bull and climb into a hot bath or you'll catch your death."

"All right," she said. His tone was friendly, but she noticed he avoided her eyes.

"Same goes for you, Dick," Phil went on. "Drop in at Brookfield and get fixed up. Ask Mum for some of my clothes." He made for the door. "I'm going to break the news to Fairbrother. Then I'll go down and report to the police."

"Give you a lift, Jane?" Dick straightened up after scraping some of the mud from his trousers. "Are you brave enough to sit on the pillion of my motor-bike?"

"Just about." She turned to thank him. He gave her a quizzical, yet strangely penetrating, glance. "Eventful evening, eh, Jane?" When she nodded, he asked, "Too crowded for you to take another shock?"

There can't be any more, she thought—not worse than I've already had.

"Go ahead," she said.

From his pocket Dick pulled a ragged, triangular piece of rough tweed to which was sewn a coat button.

"I tore this off that joker I was chasing tonight," he said quietly, dangling the scrap of material before her eyes. "What's more, I know damn well who he is."

Her tawny eyes widened in surprise.

"You know?"

"I'm reasonably sure."

"Then why on earth didn't you say?"

He did not reply immediately. First he folded the cloth and stowed it away carefully in an inside pocket, then took her arm and led her to the door.

"Because it's someone we're all more or less tied up with," he said soberly. "If I opened my trap the whole affair would become embarrassingly and hopelessly involved—for all of us. Trust me to get a lovely story I can't possibly use! If I did do anything about it, I'd never dare come near Ambridge again—I'd be outcast number one. Too bad, isn't it?"

XV

PHIL heard the motor-bike plunge down the drive as he walked through the door and found his employer having a nightcap in front of the study fire. Fairbrother's guests had gone and his expression suggested he had spent a pleasant and successful evening. He was relaxed and comfortable, a man in command of himself and in control of the situation around him.

"What on earth d'you want to see me about at this time of night, Philip?"

He put down the book he was reading and listened attentively as Phil told him about the attempt to sabotage the drill motor.

"We muffed the whole thing, Mr. Fairbrother. I'm sorry. Anyway, I'll go straight down and report to the police," Phil concluded rather lamely. He felt slightly ashamed of himself for having failed to achieve any results.

Fairbrother's expression hardened. "It was a demonstration brought about by the public enquiry, I suppose."

"More than likely, sir," Phil said non-committally. He knew that he was now on dangerous ground.

"Pity you didn't catch 'em. I'd have made an example of 'em." Suddenly and sharply he looked up. "Or perhaps you knew that?" For a moment, in his haunted and vulnerable look, there was a fleeting resemblance to Grace.

"We didn't let 'em escape on purpose, sir, if that's what you're thinking," Phil said quietly. "I mightn't see eye to eye with you on the ironstone scheme, but as long as I'm your farm manager I'll try to do the job conscientiously—and that includes safeguarding your property."

"Good." Fairbrother's eyes studied him closely, and his expression relaxed. "Have a drink before you go." This, for him, was an offer of friendship and trust. He reached out for the whisky bottle and the neat spirit warmed Phil's cold mouth and lifted from his mind some of the feeling of defeat which had oppressed him.

A few minutes later Phil excused himself.

"Time I went, sir. The policeman'll be in bed if I don't get a move on."

He closed the study door quietly behind him and limped across the hall. He had the front door half open when a voice behind him called softly, "Phil!"

Grace was a vision of beauty at the foot of the stairs.

She was still in the gleaming white off-the-shoulder gown and the sight of her brought back to him with a rush the disturbing intensity of her effect on his emotions in the farm office a couple of hours earlier. Confused, he felt he wanted to dash out of the door—to run away from an encounter he was not ready to face; but something held him there fascinated, watching her come towards him. Tonight he was at the mercy of his inflamed emotions.

He half started across the hall to meet her, but a stab of pain in his ankle brought back the memory of Jane— Jane soaking wet and muddy, kneeling beside him in the field while she examined his ankle, pleading with him in a broken voice not to become involved with Grace.

The warmth of his gaze brought a flush the colour of dawn from the hollow at the base of her throat up over her chin to her cheeks and thence across her wide forehead. In this moment of uncertainty and leashed desire she was unbelievably lovely. Phil's breath caught and he took another pace towards her.

His hands went out to her bare shoulders and he gently fondled her neck.

"There's been so much happening," he said. "I— I'm a bit confused. I don't know my own mind. Forgive me for everything, my dear." He sounded humble, weary. "I—I can't talk to you properly yet, Grace. I haven't had time to think . . . and I suppose the hurting thing is that I do need time to think."

"I can wait," she whispered, her mouth warm and soft against his ear.

Gratefully he brushed her shoulder with his lips and went out into the night. His head felt light and full of dreams, but his shoulders were slumped and his weary, aching foot dragged behind him like a burden.

It was three or four days later that Dan Archer said to Doris:

"What's up with our Phil? What's worrying him? Something seems to have bowled him over all of a sudden."

They had driven back to Brookfield from a choir practice in the school to find Phil spreadeagled in an armchair in the front room, feet on the mantelpiece, toasting himself by the fire. He was so deep in thought he barely noticed Dan look into the room for a few moments before he joined Doris in the kitchen.

"He hasn't told me anything." Doris busied herself with a tray of supper things while Dan made up the range for the night. The clatter of cups counterpointed the homely thud of coke. "I know he was disappointed they didn't catch the saboteurs the other night."

"There's more to it than that, I reckon."

They had supper around the fire in the sitting-room, drawing Phil into their conversation when they could. He seemed disinclined to talk much. Only when Doris said, "Sit up, boy, or you'll get indigestion!" did he rouse himself and lower his feet from the mantelpiece.

"What's up, lad?" Dan asked. "Something on your mind?"

"In a way." Phil dusted some crumbs off his lap and stood up. "Been thinking about putting the notion to a girl that we get married."

Dan and Doris exchanged a significant glance. So that was it—they might have guessed!

"Can you afford it, son?" asked Dan cagily.

"Could you when you took the jump?" retorted Phil.

Dan chuckled.

"No. I still can't, either. Have to give up the old lady. Send her out to work."

"Phil." Doris looked at her son towering above her. "Let us into the secret. Who are you thinking of marrying?"

He did not reply at once, but stood jingling the coins in his pocket and biting his lower lip.

"Well," he said at last, "maybe Grace."

"But I thought you and Jane——" Dan started. Doris shot a warning look at him and he left the sentence unfinished. He went on, "At least Grace's father would offer you your own farm."

"Yes, that complicates it too," Phil said quietly. "Altogether I'm in one hell of a mess."

"And you don't know your own mind?"

"No—not yet."

Dan scratched his ear reflectively with the stem of his pipe.

"There's not much your mother and I can say, Phil. It's your decision—only for God's sake make the right 'un. Don't want to say anything that might influence you either way, lad." He lit his pipe, tamped it down with his forefinger and puffed for a few seconds to get it going. "Don't go rushing into anything until you're absolutely certain your mind's made up. And don't let Grace's money influence you. It's natural for a young fellow your age to start thinking of settling down, but first, lad, make up your mind who the girl is to be. And wait until the village is out of all this ironstone trouble."

When Phil had gone to bed Doris said, "He doesn't act much like a prospective bridegroom, does he?"

"I think he's got his head screwed on right, though," Dan replied. "And I wouldn't mind betting he begs off making a decision for quite a while."

The next day there was rain—and it rained on and off for weeks, steady, chilling winter rain that had the ditches full, the gateways like bogs and the fields pock-marked with deep indentations made in the soft ground by the hooves of cattle. Then it froze hard.

There was ice to be broken every morning in the drinking troughs, fodder to be scattered through the fields to eke out the winter grazing, young cattle to be protected from the weather. Those were the mornings when the breath condensed in a foggy cloud in front of the eyes and the touch of metal was so cold it seemed to burn; when the herons came in from the frozen, still waters to fish for trout in the Ambridge stream. Those were the nights when rats raided cornsheds and poultry stores in search of food; when the mad laughter of wild geese in the young wheat mingled with the yapping of a dog fox venturing far from home.

It was a time of muddy boots and running noses, chapped hands and chafed wrists—a gloomy time made more depressing by the fact that every day brought nearer the verdict of the public enquiry on the iron-stone scheme.

"Cold enough to freeze your thoughts before you can think 'em," Simon said.

It did seem that way, Dan conceded. It was as though everything was in cold storage—suspended. There were no more attempts at sabotage. The police made no progress in tracing the saboteurs. Phil did nothing about his own problems, but avoided any close contact with Grace or Jane and doggedly went about his work.

Simon was right, Dan thought. The whole blessed thing was on ice. There was no warmth in the village left. Only a stony, bitter uncertainty.

One afternoon Mr. Crawford returned to Ambridge. Dan and Walter Gabriel were chatting just before milking time in the yard at Brookfield when they saw Crawford's big car coming up the road.

"Hey up, Dan," Walter rasped. "Here's the feller hisself. Come to start countin' the tons of iron with old Fairy Brother, more than likely."

Bill Slater was bringing the cows in for milking from the pasture on the opposite side of the road from the yard gate. Daisy, the leader, was already in the yard, with the rest of the herd trailed out leisurely behind her across the road and into the field beyond. Crawford pulled up a few yards from the unhurried cows and sat with engine idling, waiting for Bill to hold up the stream and let him through; but the youth made no attempt to do so. After a sullen look of recognition he turned his back on Crawford and allowed the cows to carry on.

"Hey!" Dan was striding across the yard. "Can't you see there's a car waiting?"

"Yes—and he can go on waiting," Bill retorted.

Dan crossed the road and held the rest of the cows at the field gate. Crawford brought the car forward a few yards and paused long enough to say: "Thanks, Mr. Archer. The ironstone scheme still provokes bad feeling, eh?"

"And bad manners by the look of it. Bill's a young fool."

"The same chap who threatened Fairbrother in the pub that night, isn't it?"

When Dan nodded Crawford gave him a brief smile and let in the clutch. "I'd better move on while I'm still all in one piece."

When he was back in the yard Dan said roughly:

"What the devil did you want to do a thing like that for?"

"He could have waited. We don't owe him anything," Bill said. "He's not Gawd A'mighty."

With a truculent shrug he went off to get his milking smock. Walter regarded his retreating figure and shook his head sadly.

"The boy seems to have a grudge against everybody —including hisself," he observed.

"If it wasn't for upsetting Peggy and Mrs. Perkins I'd have got rid of him long ago," Dan said.

"Not sure as it would upset 'em overmuch, me old pal," Walter grunted. "They're fed up with him too."

"Gambling and boozing still, is he?"

"Ay. Young fool don't know when he's well off."

Blessed awkward, Dan thought. Take sympathy on a chap when he's been working in a factory and got something the matter with his chest; give him an open-air job so he can mend and what happens? He gets in with the wrong lot—a hot-headed, scatter-brained, discontented lot of young scallywags—loses interest in his job and lets you down. And blames everybody but himself for his own shortcomings.

If it wasn't for the fact that Bill was kind of related . . .

"He wants a man around to leather his backside now and again." Walter ran his hand across the grey stubble on his chin. "If you don't take it on I shall have to. You got more cause than me."

"What d'you mean, Walter?"

There was a long pause, while Walter thought. Dan had time to look up at the pattern in the sky, a luminous shot-silk of orange and pink, deep at the horizon and paling almost to white overhead, in fronds of far-flung cirrus. One part of Dan's mind registered the fleeting loveliness of the pattern of cloud and a more practical part warned him that it would be windy on the morrow.

"Didn't you know," Walter was saying, "that Bill tried a bit o' hanky-panky with Christine some time back?"

"Oh, did he!" Grimly Dan turned on his heel and strode into the cowshed.

Walter lingered, listening, still a little dubious about the wisdom of having reported the lad. By the time Dan had finished telling Bill what he thought of him, Walter was almost sorry for the boy.

Had it coming to him, though, he reflected. Had it coming a long time.

He fingered his heavy belt, remembering the rough-and-ready ministerings of his grandmother, who had brought him up.

Walter knew that in a district where "characters" of various kinds abounded in plenty, he himself was considered a character beyond compare. And though many would scoff and groan good-humouredly when they heard Walter start a discourse with the words, "My old grannie allus used to say . . .", those who knew the true circumstances realised why he used the phrase so often and how genuinely he missed the old lady, even though he was now fifty-eight.

What farming he knew he had learnt from her instruction rather than from text-books and, although by the modern standards of Phil Archer his methods might be pretty sketchy, Walter refused to alter them. What was good enough for his old grannie was good enough for him—and though her farming knowledge may have been a fraction inadequate, her standards of conduct and living were not. Her manners had been good, too, and many a reddened ear and spinning head had reminded her grandchild that he was expected to grow into one of nature's gentlemen.

The lessons had not been forgotten in the passing of the years. Although Walter's hat was fairly held to be the most disreputable in the village, when he met a lady it was invariably swept off with all the courtly grace of a cavalier doffing his plumed headgear. He himself would never have held up a car for cows. A cantankerous, gossiping old scallywag people might call him, but at heart Walter believed himself to be a gentleman, unobtrusively kind and helpful to the weak and the needy, always ready to stop work for a pint or a chat but just as ready to waste two hours mending the broken toy of some weeping child.

In the maudlin moments when an over-indulgence of cider or perry brought tears to his eyes, Walter could conjure up a vivid mental image of himself helping a lame dog over a stile. When the dog turned round to lick his hand in gratitude he was always wildly concerned to recognise that it had the face of his grannie. It was at moments like this he sighed for his youth and dreamed of what might have been had his wife still been alive. . . .

In the cowshed Dan was giving Bill the sharp edge of his tongue. Walter could imagine the youngster going back to Mrs. Perkins' cottage in a suppressed fury, spoiling to work off his temper on somebody. It would not be Mrs. P., Walter determined. Therefore that evening found him down at her cottage with a bag of tools, shaving a bit off a sticking door, oiling a hinge, tapping in a wall plug for the good lady to hang a picture, while he waited for the youth to come in and start something. But Bill did not come.

In due course Mrs. Perkins expressed her thanks to the self-appointed handyman in a pile of hot scones which he proceeded to demolish.

"Your young rascal," said Walter, mouth full and butter running down his chin, "'e seems to be getting bad again. Dan give 'im a piece of 'is tongue this afternoon."

Mrs. Perkins, hovering, watching Walter, said, "I dunno, to be sure. Wonder 'e wasn't sacked. And where is he now? Down at the Bull, more than likely. Grumbling and carrying on, too, I'll bet. Never met such a boy for grumbling. Doesn't know which side his bread's buttered."

Walter demolished another scone, licked his greasy fingers delicately and winked.

"I do, though, ma'am," he said. "I do."

XVI

JANE MAXWELL's usual weekly letter from her mother was waiting for her when she got back to the Bull after her long day's work. Old Sam, the landlord—never reliable at taking phone messages—said Dick Raymond had rung.

"Summat about being told by his boss to do a job at short notice, miss. Summat about might not be able to meet you—or summat."

"All right, Sam. Thanks."

Another empty evening. She was not particularly disappointed about Dick. She had gone out with him once or twice to try and get him to tell her who was responsible for the sabotage. It helped to occupy her mind and forget her uncertainty while Phil was still so remote and casual. But she could not so much as flirt with Dick when her heart was still weighted with longing for Phil.

At first she had wild fears that Grace might be behind the sabotage, paying someone to try and wreck the scheme because she realised that if it went through she might never get Phil. Later, in saner moments, Jane realised that this notion was fantastic. Dick refused to be drawn, however, and now she was losing interest in him. Funny, this. Before she had met Phil she had enjoyed the company and the kisses of nearly every man who came her way. But lately, there was only one man in the world.

She bathed, changed and had her meal before she settled with her mother's letter. It cheered her a little but not much.

"*Your father and I are a little worried because you sounded rather depressed in your last letter. Perhaps it was the weather. It's been atrocious and it must be quite a trial for you working out of doors these days . . .*"

It doesn't help, Jane agreed.

"*We don't know where you get your energy and determination from to stick it like that—certainly not us . . .*"

They were a gay pair, fond of parties and social life. Her mother had been brought up to believe that the best people never soiled their fingers with manual labour.

Lately, Jane had found work becoming more difficult. I used to do it, she thought, just for the reward of a smile of thanks or a word of encouragement from Phil— enjoyed almost knocking myself out to please him. But he's more sparing with his compliments these days—as though he's half-afraid I might misconstrue anything he says into an admission that he loves me. Well, why should I care?

"*In these days when it's almost a crime to have a bit of money of your own it's nice to think that one member of the family can't be classed as 'idle rich'. We both think you were very sensible to insist on being trained in something practical . . .*"

Mum, you're a dear to try and give my ego a little puff like that, but it isn't so simple. Just now, I couldn't care less about the land, and all the clods who work on it.

"*We wondered if you might be rather lonely living in a country inn. Have you thought of trying to get two rooms with a married couple somewhere? It might be more pleasant for you than the impersonal atmosphere of an hotel.*

"*Let me know, dear, if you get bored and want to come home, or if you want a holiday. It would be nice to go to St. Moritz for the ski-ing in February, don't you think? Remember what fun we had last year, darling! And do you remember that divine young man whose father owned a vineyard?*"

Then followed a paragraph or two about some special undies her mother had bought for her, the latest news on the health of various members of the family, and that was all.

Jane finished her coffee and went up to her room. As she passed the bar she could hear the buzz of voices inside, speculating on the reason for Crawford's return that afternoon. The topic of ironstone was on everyone's lips again.

Voices were still raised in argument nearly an hour later when she came down to post the letter she had written to her parents. She paused a moment and listened. It seemed that some time during the day Dan Archer had had a row with Bill Slater.

"He can't talk to me like that and get away with it!" Bill's harsh tones came clearly through the closed bar door.

"You deserved it." This from Simon, Dan's other employee.

"You shut up!"

"I was working for Dan Archer afore you was born," Simon said. "You won't find a better nor fairer gaffer, either. If you deserves a bawling out you gets one."

Bill cursed. It was too lurid for Jane and she moved away.

"I'll chuck it in!" she heard him say. "I'll blasted well pack up and clear off back to London, where what I do in my spare time is nobody else's business. It's a free country. I'll spend my time how I like."

Jane posted her letter in the box near the green and stood considering how to spend the rest of the evening. The loneliness of her own room back at the Bull did not attract her, nor the cheap tobacco and limited conversation of the public bar. Perhaps her mother was right. Maybe she ought to go into digs somewhere.

"All dressed up and nowhere to go?"

She looked round to see the tall form of Mrs. Perkins in the gloom.

"Hello, Mrs. P. I didn't hear you coming."

"Got me rubbers on, dear," panted the formidable old lady, breathing hard under the weight of two imitation-leather shopping bags. "Walked down the street with Mister Gabriel, then I been to the sale o' work. Bought a lot of junk as I don't want. Loaded myself up. Always do. You know how it is. Folk worked hard to raise funds for something or other. Don't like to leave it on the stalls."

"Let me help you carry something."

Jane remembered Bill's wild talk and toyed with the idea of moving in with Mrs. Perkins if he left. At least it could do no harm to have a look at the place.

"Come in for a minute and have a warm? Come and see all the jobs Mister Gabriel did for me tonight."

"Thanks, Mrs. Perkins. I'd like to."

They went into the darkened house together. The fire in the living-room was almost out and Mrs. Perkins had to grope around for the light switch.

"There. The fire's nearly out. I must have been away longer than I thought." Tut-tutting to herself, she bustled out to the back kitchen. "Drat that Bill. He hasn't filled the coal scuttle like I told him to this morning."

"I'll do it for you," Jane volunteered.

"There's a good girl. Meantime I'll try to kindle it with a bit of wood," Mrs. Perkins handed her a cycle lamp. "Mind the water butt. Watch you don't twist your ankle where the crazy paving's sunk. Duck as you go under the clothes line."

Jane smiled to herself as she negotiated the obstacles Mrs. Perkins had enumerated. She found the coal-house was a stone lean-to inconveniently situated at the rear of the cottage. It was well stocked with coal and unthinkingly she dug the shovel into the bottom of the stack. The coal started to slide, cascading out over her feet and across the path.

"Fool thing!"

She filled the scuttle and started to shovel the coal back but only succeeded in starting another slide. She was about to give up when she noticed something exposed in the pile of coal, something that gleamed under its coat of coal dust, reflecting the beam of the lamp she held.

Recognising it, but too shocked to believe her eyes, she bent forward and picked it up, rubbing away the grime.

"The drill! The stolen drill!" she whispered.

There was no mistake about it. It was the diamond cutting-head stolen from Fairbrother's drilling equipment months ago when the sabotage incidents had first started.

At once she understood why Dick Raymond wouldn't

tell her what he knew, realising how hopelessly it would involve them all.

Bill Slater! So that's who it was they both tackled in the dark that night. Bill Slater was one of the saboteurs!

She stood helplessly looking at the gleaming, beautifully-made component in her hand, trying to marshal her thoughts and work out what she was going to do.

Then quick footsteps sounded on the path behind her. She began to panic.

"Mrs. Perkins coming to see what I'm up to. What'll I tell her?" She swung round, flashing the cycle lamp along the path and trying to hold the diamond head out of sight behind her back. The beam of the lamp lit up the approaching figure and she caught her breath.

"Gimme that!"

There was a sadistic leer on his face and his arms were spread wide so that she could not push past him.

"Okay—so you won't—then I'll take it!"

He sprang without warning. The lamp shattered on the ground and his hand clamped with bruising force over her mouth, cutting off her scream for help.

In high spirits, Dick Raymond sent his motor-bike roaring past Ambridge Parish Church. He had ridden recklessly from Borchester on icy roads, anxious not to miss his date with Jane.

Throughout the journey his mind had been on girls in general and three in particular. He admired remote, cool Grace for her beauty and her dignity. She was, in his romantic mind, the symbol of the lovely unattainable who is every young man's dream and ideal. But the reality was nearer to hand in the persons of Christine and Jane—friendly girls who were easy to understand. They liked him, he knew, because he was fairly well-read, easy-going, and attentive when he cared to be.

Fair-haired Christine, with her pretty face, and her stolid, matter-of-fact acceptance of life, was the sort of girl a man could turn to in a crisis, knowing that she would console him and restore his self-confidence.

Tumultuous Jane, on the other hand, would be much more likely to lead a fellow into some ridiculous scrape which would show him up as a hero or as a prize fool. Either way, she would laugh at him and refuse to take him seriously. Dick could, he imagined, become very fond of Jane. She had a wide, sensuous mouth—the sort he could become a slave to if he had any intention of becoming emotionally ensnared by any one girl at this stage of his career.

He parked his motor-bike against the old stone mounting block in front of the Bull, switched off his lights and went in the main entrance. Sam, the land-lord, was collecting empty glasses from the tiny shelf in the passage.

"Didn't expect to see you tonight," Sam said.

Beneath his warm leather jacket Dick's heart plunged downwards. When he had telephoned earlier, he had been insistent that Sam get a message to Jane, but Sam had seemed abstracted, as if he were really listening to some other conversation. He was sensible enough normally, but the very act of lifting a telephone receiver seemed to drive all wits from Sam's bald head. Once before, when he had failed to pass on a message, Sam had heard the sharp edge of Dick's tongue. The landlord's only excuse was that pub-keepers were not trained to use the phone. The police might be listening, and it was his practice to be mysterious and brief.

Tonight Dick was not surprised, therefore, when Sam went on:

"Her's gone out. You said you wasn't coming."

Useless to tell Sam he had the message wrong, the reporter thought. He asked, "Any idea where she's gone?"

Big, florid and unhurried, his massive hands clutching a dozen glasses, Sam eased the bar door open with his stomach.

"Seen Jane?" he boomed. "Young Mister Raymond's here for her."

At the bar were Phil, Walter and Dan. Phil waved a greeting and grinned.

"D'you mean Jane or Chris, eh, Dick?"

At once the young reporter was embarrassed. He saw the quizzical look in Dan Archer's eyes and coloured up with a flush of annoyance when Walter Gabriel, a knowing twist to his mouth, rasped:

"Saw her and Mrs. Perkins going into Mrs. P.'s cottage less than five minutes ago." Walter managed to see and to remember nearly everything.

"Thanks."

Dick turned abruptly and left the pub, anxious to avoid any further comment and leg-pulling by the three men.

Outside he kicked irritably at the starter of his motorbike, taking out on it the anger he felt at Sam's incompetence. He had given up Press tickets to a Felpersham theatre tonight in order to come to Ambridge to see Jane, and it was quite infuriating to find that she did not even know he was here.

His ill-temper was still with him when he reached

Mrs. Perkins' cottage. Again he succumbed to the temptation to take it out of the bike and, deftly bringing it through the gate, accelerated hard up the path at the side of the cottage. At the last moment he cut his engine and slammed on his brakes, slewing the machine round to a broadsiding halt by the water butt.

"What the——?"

His anger was gone, replaced by sudden amazement. The beam of the headlight, swinging over the neat little kitchen garden and along the rear of the house, lit up for a brief instant two struggling figures near the coalhouse.

Already half off the machine, Dick wrenched the handlebars round to bring the light on the couple again. Racing along the path, he had a fleeting impression of Jane's coal-streaked, terrified face buffeted and trapped by the flailing arms of Bill Slater.

Then he moved into the attack. The impetus of his rush sent Bill stumbling back, clutching at Jane to keep his balance. The girl twisted away from his fingers and he clawed helplessly at the air, body arched back and arms windmilling wildly.

Coal rolled away from under Bill's staggering feet. For a brief instant he floundered, then crashed back into the coalhouse.

His head met the wall with a thud.

The reporter pulled Jane behind him and stood with fists bunched. Bill struggled dizzily to his feet, clutching at the doorpost for support. He seemed blinded by the motor-cycle headlight and brought his forearm up to mask his face, in anticipation of Dick's attack.

For a second the reporter's attention was diverted by the gleaming drill component lying on the path. The youth lurched out of the headlight's beam and stumbled away in the darkness around the other side of the cottage.

"I found the drill in the coal," Jane panted. "Bill saw me."

They heard the back door open a few yards away round the angle of the wall and Mrs. Perkins' voice raised in inquiry.

"Who is it? Was that Mr. Raymond's bike I just heard?"

"What are we going to do?" Jane asked in a whisper.

Dick bent down, picked up the drill component and hid it under his heavy waterproof.

"Jane!" There was anxiety in Mrs. Perkins' voice.

"It's all right. Dick's helping me with the coal. It tumbled out!"

Mrs. Perkins appeared at the corner.

"Tt-tt-tt-tt. What a muddle you've got yourselves in," she observed. "Coal all over the place."

"We won't be a couple of shakes." Jane's attempt to sound cheerful gave her voice a high, unnatural note. "We'll tidy up while Dick's still got his headlight on." As soon as Mrs. Perkins went into the house, the girl repeated in a whisper: "What are we going to do, Dick? Should we tell her?"

"Blessed if I know."

The reporter slipped the drill component into the saddlebag of his motor-bike and returned to Jane. She had started to fill the scuttle and when he took the shovel from her, he took her warm, grubby hand and found that her fingers trembled as they tightened impulsively round his, as if to draw strength and reassurance from his grip.

"You all right?" he asked.

"It's—it's just the shock."

"Of the fight?"

"And finding out about Bill." In her agitation her voice grew in volume. "Dick, he's been doing it, hasn't he—the sabotage?"

He said nothing but attacked the coal on the path, shovelling it vigorously back into the stack, finding relief in the physical effort, released from the disturbing intimate grip of her fingers.

"What are we going to do now, Dick?"

"Act as though nothing had happened. Don't let on to Mrs. Perkins. We'll get away as soon as we can."

When they got into the house Mrs. Perkins was on her knees before the sitting-room fire, beating out sparks that leaped on to the rug from the blaze of wood in the grate.

"Young folk seem to be like children nowadays," she grunted. Her acid tone and severe expression was belied by the amused twinkle in her eye. "Give 'em a simple job to do and they get messed up to the eyebrows." Banking up the fire with coal, she jerked her head in the direction of the kitchen door. "Better wash yourselves. Towel's on the back door."

It was when Dick reached with dripping hands for the towel that he noticed the old tweed jacket hanging on the door. Flipping it around on its loop so that the buttons were visible, he dug into his inside pocket and brought out the scrap of cloth he had shown Jane weeks before on the night they had helped to foil the saboteurs. Silently he drew her attention to the fact that the piece of material, with the button, was missing.

"Bill's jacket," he whispered. "That, I think, just about proves it."

The girl gave him a warning nudge, and when Mrs.

Perkins came into the kitchen they were both apparently absorbed in drying their hands.

"You'll have a cup of something hot, of course," she said, busying herself with the kettle. "You must have something to keep the cold out."

They could not escape for fear of offending her or arousing her suspicions. Somehow they kept abreast of her conversation, laughing and joking about Jane's clumsiness with the coal, but it was half an hour before they were able to make their excuses and get away.

"Let's walk," Dick said. "I'll collect the bike later."

"The drill——?"

"It'll be all right in my saddlebag. I can't see Bill showing himself back here until he's found out what we've done."

"What *are* we going to do?" Jane asked for the fourth time. Without waiting for his answer, she went on: "I never suspected him, because that night Fairbrother called the meeting—d'you remember?—it was Bill who gave the alarm when Fairbrother's ricks were fired. That was crafty."

They turned into the road and set off towards the Bull.

"You realize now why I couldn't open my mouth," Dick said. "Besides, at that time I only suspected the truth. I didn't have proof."

Jane walked on in silence for a while.

"It's so awful for Phil—for Chris—for all the Archers," she said at last. "Dick, is it wrong to keep information like this to ourselves?"

"It might be."

"We won't say anything," Jane said with sudden determination. "The repercussions would be too awful. We'll keep it to ourselves."

"What about you, though?" Dick drew her arm through his own. "He might get tough again."

She thought for a moment.

"I don't think he will. He won't risk me splitting."

Two of us have decided independently to keep quiet, thought Dick. Maybe it would be the best thing to do, if they could be sure the sabotage would not continue. Bill and his cronies would probably lie low until the truth was out.

"Wonder where the blighter slunk off to afterwards? I ought to have poked him one instead of just shoving him off you."

Ahead of them, on the road near the green, a light appeared. Thinking a cyclist approached, Dick drew the girl closer to the verge, but almost at once he realized from the way the light danced that it came from a torch held in someone's hand. Silhouetted against the light, a small knot of shadowy people were grouped around a shapeless figure lying in the road.

Unconsciously Jane and Dick quickened their pace.

"What's happened?"

"It's all right." Dan Archer's voice, steady and calm, came out of the gloom surrounding the torch. "The doctor's been phoned for."

Dick forced his way between Walter Gabriel and Phil and looked down at the figure lying on the fringe of the green.

"Oh, my God! Jane!" He dragged her after him through the circle of men. "It's Bill!"

The youth lay crumpled on his side, arms and legs angled as though he had fallen, tried to rise again and toppled sideways. His hands were black with coal dust. Some of it had been transferred to his pallid hollow-cheeked face; greyish-black streaks across his forehead and temples and smudges across his closed eyes and his cheeks that gave his features the appearance of a skull.

Walter's overcoat was thrown over him and Phil's rolled scarf was under his head.

"Best not to move him till the doctor gets here," Walter suggested.

"We found him lying here when we came out of the Bull," Phil explained. "We almost tripped over him, too."

"Car must've knocked him for six by the look of it," Dan said.

"No," Dick interrupted quietly. "It wasn't a car. I socked him." He sensed the tension in the men grouped round him and felt Jane's fingers grip his arm. "It was at Mrs. Perkins'—half an hour ago. Bill was going for Jane—near the coalhouse. Then—I—I——"

Phil shone the torch into his face, half blinding him.

"That's quite true," Jane cut in quickly. "I was getting some coal when Bill came for me. Dick arrived and pushed him off and—and he went away somewhere. We—we didn't want to worry Mrs. Perkins, so we said nothing."

An inarticulate growl expressing disgust and anger rumbled in Walter's throat.

"Hanky-panky again, eh? Tried the same trick wi' young Jane as he did wi' Chris."

"Again?" Dan sounded incredulous. "After that blowing-up I gave him?"

"Just the sort of damfool thing he would do, ain't it? To show his independence. And remember what Sam said about him being in the pub shouting his head off with big talk earlier on?"

Dick opened his mouth to speak again, but a warning pressure of Jane's hand on his arm silenced him.

Anxiously Phil turned to the girl.

"Are you all right, Jane? He didn't——"

"No—Dick arrived."

The approach of the doctor's car put an end to their conversation. They stood apart while the doctor brought his headlights to bear on the unconscious figure and they waited in silence while he made his examination.

Dick prayed silently that the boy would be all right, blaming himself for what had happened. He remembered all too vividly Bill stumbling over the coals and the sickening hollow thud of the back of his head striking the wall. There was also, he remembered, a long history of bronchial and asthmatic trouble which had weakened Bill's constitution. Looking down at the unconscious figure, Dick was wrenched by sympathy and remorse. He should not have socked the fellow quite so hard.

The doctor looked up from his examination.

"Could someone phone for an ambulance?" he said, professionally unmoved. "He'll have to go to hospital. Seems like a severe concussion."

XVII

THE MORNING sun came through strong for December, giving an unusual brilliance to the frost-clothed countryside. Standing at the window of Fairbrother's breakfast-room, looking across the meadows to the woods surrounding the Manor, Henry Crawford could feel the warmth of the sun's rays on his face. It gave him a warm sense of pleasure and well-being.

Crawford had mellowed of late. He had found out a week ago that he had been elected to the board of an aluminium company and he had a sense of achievement in the unexpected acquisition of so much power.

All his life he had gathered power to himself, finding that the more he had, the more he wanted.

Now he had enough. Aluminium, not iron, he believed, was the mineral of the modern age. He visualised, as he looked out of Fairbrother's window, great new empires of influence. He would make his power felt among the manufacturers of aircraft, the makers of office equipment, kitchenware distributors—everywhere. There would not be a household in Great Britain from which Crawford would not receive unconscious tribute, because no home would be without aluminium.

He had time, now, to stand and stare. He could relax and smile at the flowing landscape.

Before his eyes was the rose garden, beautiful even in its bare twigs and thorns because it gave promise of loveliness. The brick garden wall was speckled with winter jasmine, which glowed like daylight stars. Above, the sky was pale but clear with the brilliance of the shell of a pearl. It seemed to curve downwards to the fallow winter landscape and the neatly ploughed rich dark earth, waiting expectantly for seed-time.

"There's a lot to be said for living in the country," he said, contrasting the bustle surrounding his London flat with the peaceful scene outside. "You Fairbrothers have the right idea. This is just the place to relax from the cares and worries of our so-called civilization."

Grace Fairbrother joined him at the window. "And how long will it stay that way?" she asked very quietly.

The sun played on Crawford's dark hair when he turned to her. His eyes regarded her with an expression that was almost benevolent.

"Are you still worried about the ironstone?"

"Very."

Last night there had been discussion between Crawford and Fairbrother about getting in a mining contractor to survey the scheme and make practical suggestions how the ironstone was to be mined. Fairbrother seemed to think they could manage on their own.

"I disagree," Crawford had said. "Let's have a practical man on the job. Give the contract to an experienced man and let him do the day-to-day worrying on our behalf. Besides, he'll have all the necessary plant and equipment."

Fairbrother had seen the sense in that. He had also made a few pointed remarks about getting their agreement on the mineral rights completed.

"You two are behaving as though the public-enquiry

verdict had already been announced in your favour,"
Grace had said.

"It will be," her father had replied with quiet
assurance.

Going over the events of the previous evening as he
gazed out of the window, Crawford admitted to himself
that Fairbrother was probably right.

He himself had gathered from the transcript of the
evidence given at the public enquiry that approval of
the scheme was almost certain.

He became conscious that Grace was regarding him
intently. "I know! You want to ask some awkward
questions."

She nodded.

"Why are you taking so long to sign the agreement
with Daddy on the mineral rights?"

Crawford's brow wrinkled and he fished in his pocket
for a cigarette.

"You think I'm putting something over on him?"

"No, I don't. You're not the sort. But I *would*
like to know the real reason."

"I don't know it myself. Perhaps it's because I'm
not sure yet that the scheme's a desirable thing. Perhaps because there's no point in putting the cart before
the horse and getting everything signed up before we
know the verdict."

The sun went in behind the high cloud and, suddenly restless, he left the window to pace around the
room.

"No, I don't know, Grace. Maybe I'm naturally
cautious. Maybe there's an unsuspected streak of
sentiment in me that finds a soft spot for Ambridge.
Maybe, if you will excuse me for seeming blunt and
tactless, my mind is on matters which will pay greater

dividends for a great deal less work. I just don't know."
He paused, flicked the cigarette he'd barely started into
the grate. "D'you want me to sign?"

A metallic clatter broke the silence that followed the
business man's staccato inquiry. At the door of the
implement shed across the yard, visible to Crawford and
Grace through the window, Phil Archer was cranking
the heavy tractor.

"You know the answer as well as I do," Grace said.

When Phil Archer got home to tea that evening Mrs.
Perkins and Walter Gabriel were there, fresh from a
visit to the hospital to see Bill Slater.

"Still unconscious," Walter reported. "Don't look
too good, neither."

"Blest if I know what we're going to do with him
when he comes out," Dan was saying. "He can't go on
like he has been doing. Our Chris and then Jane. . . ."

Christine stared at her plate, flushed and embarrassed.

"If I hadn't turned up first time and young Dick the
second, there's no knowing what would've happened,"
Walter rasped. "Though I'll allow I can make a pretty
shrewd guess."

"He's a very bad boy," Mrs. Perkins said.

"I know he's your nephew, Mrs. P.," Doris said.
"But I'm afraid I wouldn't be happy with him about
the place after—after what's happened."

"Soon as he's well we'll pack him off back to London." The angular widow spoke with an air of quiet
determination. "He's fouled his nest here."

The talk flowed on. Phil, sensing Christine's unhappiness over the incident, gave his sister's shoulder
a reassuring squeeze as he passed to go to the dresser.

A sudden flame of anger flared up in him when he

thought that Grace too might have been victim to one of Bill Slater's attacks.

Every time he thought of Grace, and it was frequently these days, he was filled with protective tenderness and an anxious care for her welfare. As he mused about her loveliness, the others continued to talk about the invalid.

"Might improve the lad, y'know." Walter's harsh voice topped the general talk. "This shake-up might do him as much good as a right old larruping."

"It might." Doris reached across the table for their empty cups. "Dan says Dick was very worried because he felt he was responsible. It's such a shame."

Phil tried to bring his thoughts back to the discussion, but an insistent questioning that had gone unanswered over the past weeks occupied him.

There was no use in his saying anything about his feelings when he had nothing to offer Grace except the prospect of trying to grow crops on top of a mine. His instinct was to speak; what held him back was the fact that he knew her father would offer him, as casually as offering a cigar, a farm of his own as a wedding present.

That was the danger about Grace. . . . Phil's feelings for her were mixed up with his desire for land and security. He wanted his own farm, but he wanted to earn it the hard way, with his own hands and brains. Marrying the daughter of the wealthiest man in the district before he had property of his own would destroy his independence. As Fairbrother's farm manager, he was free, the master of his own fate. As Fairbrother's penniless son-in-law, he would be merely a property like a tractor.

Phil admitted ruefully to himself that he was as

proud as Grace. In his case, pride must outweigh love, or he would have told her long ago just how precious she was to him. . . .

The telephone rang and Dan went into the passage to answer it.

After a few words, Phil watched his father cover the mouthpiece with his hand, heard him say quietly over his shoulder, "Dick Raymond."

"Eh? What's that? What news?" The farmer's serious expression deepened as he listened. "By gum, that's bad. But thanks, Dick."

Back in the kitchen, Dan looked soberly at the group round the table.

"Ministry of Town and Country Planning have reached their decision. Fairbrother can go ahead with his blessed ironstone scheme."

Everybody except Phil started to talk at once. For Phil the news came with such impact that it seemed to knock the breath out of him. He saw the results of the verdict—the despoiling of Fairbrother's farm, the destruction of the farming system he, as manager, had built up into an efficient and productive machine. Wasted years. An urge to break away and make a fresh start swept over him.

He slipped unseen from the kitchen, leaving the others to their heated discussion of the public-enquiry verdict. Phil had something important to say. His mind was made up at last.

But the icy wind sweeping across the fields seemed to tighten like a band around his forehead, squeezing out and freezing the sudden resolve that had sent him hurrying from the house. His steps faltered and when he got to a stile he stood for a minute, undecided whether to go on or to turn back. Across the valley a light burned in one of the downstairs windows of Fairbrother's house. He watched it until the cold of the earth crept up through the soles of his shoes, until the flesh in the small of his back tightened and shook uncontrollably as the wind cut through his jacket.

Numbed, he turned and wandered aimlessly back towards Brookfield, uncertain of everything but the cold without and within him.

The news that Fairbrother had planning permission to go ahead with his opencast mine spread over the village like a pall. Jane Maxwell, who had hated all thought of the scheme at first, now found herself secretly happy. She believed that Phil would never become reconciled with Grace now. By bulldozing the scheme through, the Fairbrothers had alienated themselves.

Jane understood Phil's mixed loyalties while the issue was in doubt. But now his reserve of the past few weeks would be gone. He would no longer be studiously cool.

She hurried to work, excited at the prospect of finding a new, clearer-headed Phil—a Phil she could claim for her own now the die was cast.

He was leaving the house as she entered the farm-yard, but he did not come to greet her. Instead he turned in between a couple of the buildings, and she watched him go to different vantage points in the yard —steps, fences, gates—looking out over the fields, searching.

She intercepted him by the implement sheds.

"Phil—someone has told me the news about the scheme——"

"Yes, I heard last night."

There was none of the warmth in his tone that she

expected and she forced herself to swallow her disappointment.

"Have you seen Grace at all?" he asked coldly. "I want to talk to her."

Startled, Jane looked up into his face. He kept his head turned away and she could see only the profile. His mouth and jaw were set and his brows were down, firm, unyielding. Wildly she thought of sending him to the opposite end of the farm so that he should not see Grace; but she knew at once that it would be useless.

"As I came up, I saw her over by the kale—with her father and Crawford and another man. The mining contractor, I suppose."

"Thanks." He turned away and walked towards the fence.

"Phil!" Her voice shrilled, then broke under the sudden outburst. But its urgency stopped him in his tracks.

"What the dickens——"

"Phil, listen!" She ran to his side. "Please wait!" Now she had stopped him her mind was blank. Then, in a flash of inspiration, she remembered Bill Slater. "I—I didn't want to tell you this, Phil. Dick and I agreed to say nothing, but—I think you should know."

"You mean you and Dick are——?" he began.

Seeing his brow clear and realising he thought she was trying to tell him that she and Dick had fallen in love, she fought to stop herself breaking into hysterical laughter.

"No, no." The words came in a tumbling rush. "I mean about Bill Slater. You've got to know what really happened. I found the diamond drill-head—the one that was stolen—hidden in Mrs. Perkins' coal."

"What!"

"Bill saw me with it, realised the truth was out and came for me. Dick arrived just in time."

Phil gaped. "But—you're suggesting he had something to do with the sabotage!"

"I'm afraid so. Dick was pretty certain some weeks ago—that night when we waited for them in the field—when they were going to wreck the drill motor."

"How did he find out?"

"He tackled Bill—recognised him," Jane went on.

"Strewth. This is a hell of a situation." Phil sat down on a paraffin drum, hands on his knees, eyes closed.

"Dick and I decided not to say anything—in view of you and Chris—everybody—but I thought you should know."

For a minute or two he sat in silence, turning the problem over in his mind. Then, abruptly, he was on his feet.

"Fairbrother's got to know," he said. "Over by the kale, you say?"

She nodded and watched him swing himself lithely over the fence and set off at a brisk pace across the field. A triumphant warmth rose in her. Whatever he had been thinking about Grace when she first joined him was now forgotten. It was when she remembered that Grace was with her father in the kale that Jane climbed swiftly over the fence and ran to catch up with Phil.

"I suddenly thought, Phil, if you're going to tell Fairbrother, I'd better come along, too, to corroborate," she said.

The Fairbrothers and Crawford had soon discovered that short, stocky, energetic William Lenton was a taciturn man and a chain-smoker. He tramped around the fields in thoughtful silence. Occasionally he asked a question in his rich Yorkshire accent but offered no comment on the replies. It was after he had lit what Grace estimated to be his fortieth cigarette that Lenton stood for a long while looking towards the high ground in the direction of Hollerton.

"Maps, please." It was the first time he had spoken for ten minutes. Fairbrother took the roll of maps from under his arm and spread them out.

When he had finished his examination of the maps Lenton said, "Wait here," and trudged away towards the brow of the hill. Fairbrother regarded Crawford dubiously.

"D'you think he's all right? He doesn't seem to say much for himself. What's going on in his mind?"

"We'll know in due course, I expect," Crawford smiled.

"Dour's the word, I believe, isn't it?" Grace said.

"Very peculiar." Fairbrother rubbed his chin. "I suppose he knows what he's up to."

"He's one of the top men at his job in the country." Crawford took out his cigarette-case and offered it to Grace.

"No thanks," she said. "I couldn't—not after watching Lenton."

"He's had the mineralogist's reports, the analysis figures, the evidence at the public enquiry—everything," Crawford went on. "Don't worry. He knows his business."

"You can vouch for him personally?" asked Fairbrother.

"Absolutely. We had a long talk about the scheme before I came down here."

Lenton was at the top of the rise now. They saw him

spend some time looking to all points of the compass before he retraced his steps towards them.

Unnoticed, Phil and Jane approached the group. Phil called his employer, but, anxious to hear what Lenton would have to say on his return, Fairbrother was reluctant to give his undivided attention to his farm manager.

"What is it, Philip? Is it important?" Fairbrother asked. "Can't it wait? We're rather busy."

"I think it is important, sir," Phil said. "We've traced one of the saboteurs—at least, Jane and Dick Raymond have."

"Well done!" Fairbrother gave a nod of grim satisfaction. "I thought we'd catch up with 'em before long. Well, who is it?"

"I'm afraid it's Bill Slater, sir."

"Slater!" Fairbrother exploded.

"That's the boy who works for your father?" Crawford asked incredulously.

"He also happens to be a sort of cousin by marriage," Phil said morosely.

"Phil—I'm terribly sorry." Grace came to his side, distressed and seemingly unconscious of the other girl watching her.

"How did you find out?" Fairbrother was blunt and direct. "Let's have the facts."

"You'd better tell 'em, Jane," Phil said.

He stood back out of the group while Jane told her story. When she had finished, Fairbrother said: "We'll have to make an example of young Slater. I'm sorry, Philip, but this sabotage must be stopped."

"Don't be too hasty," Jane pleaded. "He's in hospital and the accident may bring him to his senses."

Out of the corner of his eye Phil saw Lenton rejoining the group.

The mining engineer came straight to the point.

"I've seen all I want to see, gentlemen. Now I've had a look at the country I'll tell you straight away that I'm not interested."

"What's that?" Fairbrother's jaw sagged in amazement.

"I've seen the lie of the land." Lenton's tongue wetted a fresh cigarette. "Take my advice and leave the ironstone where it is."

His words fell like a bombshell among the astounded group. Phil noticed that Crawford, apparently calmer than the rest of them, avoided Fairbrother's eye. Jane's face was a mask of unbelief. The muscles of Grace's cheeks quivered as if she were going to burst into tears. An angry flush came up from Fairbrother's neck to the roots of his hair. His fists clenched tight at his sides, crumpling the maps he held.

"You've been listening to the opposition!" he almost shouted. "They've got at you! You're in with the Squire's crowd!"

"Listen," Lenton said with deliberation. "I come from an industrial area where we're not afraid of a bit o' muck. Where there's muck there's money. It takes more than a pretty country scene to stop me fetching out a million tons of ironstone. Our blast furnaces need it. But this lot—no!"

"There's some sort of conspiracy between you!" Fairbrother swung on Crawford, his eyes dark with accusation.

"Don't be a fool!" Crawford snapped. He turned to Lenton. "What's against the scheme? Why should we drop it?"

"I don't say drop it. Postpone it—five years, maybe ten."

"What are your reasons?"

"Plenty. It'll take that time to get the machinery and plant you need. There's one bit of tackle alone that takes four and a half years to build—if you can get the steel these days."

"But dammit," Fairbrother exploded, "there's steel under our feet that'll ease the shortage!"

"Ay—it's a vicious circle," Lenton agreed. He waved in the direction of the high ground, blowing the ash off his cigarette without taking it from his lips. "Here's another snag. To shift the stuff to the blast furnaces economically, you'd need to do it by rail. Your nearest railway's Hollerton. Who can spare steel to extend railway lines? Who's got the tackle to drive a tunnel through that blasted hill?"

"There must be a way," Fairbrother thundered. "I don't accept your conclusions."

"You asked for my opinion and you've got it," Lenton said dourly. "Get any expert in the country to come here and they'll tell you the same thing—only they'll have more sense than me. They'll charge you a fee and expenses."

His mouth closed like a trap and, turning on his heel, he stumped away towards the house. Fairbrother looked round helplessly.

"Crawford—surely . . ."

The other man shrugged.

"I wouldn't argue, old man. He knows his business. If he says it won't work—it won't." Crawford's own disappointment hardly showed, because his mind was now concentrated on aluminium.

"I don't believe it. I won't have it. Good Lord,

Crawford, you can't give in as easily as that! You can't back out now, man!"

He set off angrily after Lenton. Crawford hurried to catch him up. Within seconds the two men were involved in fierce argument.

Phil recovered from the stunning effect of Lenton's verdict to realise the two girls were still there. He looked quickly from one to the other. Jane's face was lit with a glow of satisfaction and he knew she was savouring the brutal directness of Lenton's opinion. It was impossible to tell what went on behind Grace's drawn and seemingly emotionless expression. Only when he felt Jane's hand creep possessively round his arm was he stirred to action.

"Better get back to the house," he muttered and led off.

The young people followed the three men back to the yards in silence, watching Fairbrother still arguing, punctuating his words with emphatic gestures. Crawford was cool and Lenton completely unmoved.

It was then that Dan Archer came round the corner of the buildings from the drive and strode across the yard towards them. The instant he saw his father's set expression, Phil realised something was wrong. He hurried over.

"What's up, Dad?"

"Thought I'd better drop by and let you know so you'll be warned before you get home, lad," Dan said quietly. "It's young Bill."

Fairbrother stopped in the middle of what he was saying to the imperturbable Lenton and looked over his shoulder.

"Bill? Young Slater, you mean, Mr. Archer?"

"Yes." The farmer took a deep breath. "He's dead."

There was a shocked silence.

"Never came out of the coma," Dan continued. "Died half an hour ago in hospital. Thought you ought to know, Phil."

Phil nodded dumbly. At his side Jane turned away, tears in her eyes.

Fairbrother passed his hand wearily over his brow.

"It's too much," he muttered. "Too much."

"This puts a new complexion on the whole thing," Crawford said gravely. He went over to Lenton, standing apart from the others, and held out his hand. "Thanks for your help, Lenton. I'll let you know our decision."

The Yorkshireman gave him a brief, understanding nod and made for his car. Ignoring the rest of the silent figures, Crawford took Fairbrother by the arm and led him towards the house.

"Come on, old man," he said, decisively taking charge. "When we get blood on our hands, it's time we took stock."

"Crawford, I'm not listening to such nonsense: Blood on our hands!" Fairbrother walked into the house and put the roll of maps on the hall table. "It's ridiculous to suggest it. Young Slater brought it on himself."

Grace followed her father and Crawford into the sitting-room. Her father was angry, but she sensed it was because the news of Bill Slater's death had shaken him.

"I suppose what you're trying to say, Crawford, is that you want to back out. Go ahead. I can still mine the ironstone on my own property. I don't need your mineral rights."

Crawford shrugged indifferently. "And the mining engineer's verdict?" he said.

"Lenton's is only one opinion. I'm not satisfied he hasn't been approached by—by the Ambridge people."

Crawford made a sound in his throat that might have been suppressed exasperation.

"Trouble is, Fairbrother," he said, "you've put yourself out on a limb and, without realising it, you're trying to chop the tree down."

Tears welling into her eyes, Grace looked hard at Crawford in silent appeal, willing him to convince her father that he must give up the scheme. *Not just for Ambridge or Phil, but for my father and me*, she thought. *This ironstone is destroying us all, everything he and I ever had.*

Crawford seemed to grasp the silent message, for his mouth relaxed and he gave Grace a barely perceptible nod.

"Fairbrother, you're making a fool of yourself," he said decisively. "You've lost all proportion. You don't, or won't, see what's going on around you."

"Making a fool of myself?" The other man swung round from the fire in astonishment.

"Daddy, please listen to Mr. Crawford."

"I think we should regard young Slater's death as—symbolic. Symbolic of the unrest in the district." Crawford's voice carried on smoothly but with studied emphasis. "What you're doing now, Fairbrother, is letting your pride take you into a desert."

"That's my affair," Fairbrother said.

"Not entirely."

Grace felt Crawford's arm around her shoulders.

"What about Grace?" he went on. "Ask her if she's happy."

She heard her father's sharp intake of breath, forced

herself to look at him and return his half-fearful, half-defiant stare. All at once Grace was crying. She was dimly aware that Crawford's arm was no longer about her shoulders and a few seconds later she heard the door of the sitting-room quietly open and close.

Her father had slumped into an armchair and was hunched forward, looking blankly into the fire, his hands limp between his knees. The glow of the fire emphasised the deepening lines of exhaustion around his mouth and eyes. He looked spent, defeated.

"Daddy!" she whispered. "Oh, Daddy!"

She was on her knees beside him, her arms about him. She felt the momentary resistance, then heard him sigh as the tension went out of him.

"It'll be all right, Daddy. It's all going to be all right."

He stroked her hair, and at this sign of affection her tears came back, but they were tears of relief, not fear. Her father was back, no longer a stranger. She felt once again she was sure of him and, content in this as the minutes passed, allowed herself to pray that perhaps Phil, too, would be hers again.

The morning after the inquest Walter Gabriel, shaven for once and dressed in sober black, came into the kitchen at Brookfield.

"You ready, me old beauty?"

"Almost, Walter." Doris Archer flicked a few specks of dust off her navy two-piece and reached for her winter coat. "Where's Mrs. Perkins?"

"Over at my place."

"Is she all right?"

"Ay. Taking it well."

Christine came downstairs carrying a quietly

patterned silk scarf. "Here, Mum. This'll relieve it a bit. It's not too gay."

Doris accepted the scarf and turned to inspect Walter. He allowed her to straighten his black tie so that the knot hid the brass circle of his collar stud. When she started on his shiny lapels with a clothes-brush his only comment was a mild, "Mrs. P.'s been at them already."

Christine said, "What about the wreath?"

"Gone," Walter answered. "Went with the others in the 'earse at eight o'clock this morning."

"Yes, there's only ourselves to worry about on the train." Doris took a final look at herself in the mirror. "I think Mrs. P. was right to say Bill should be taken back to London. After all, it was his home."

Dan came in, kicked off his wellingtons and reached for his boots.

"You folks almost ready?" he asked. "Train leaves at a quarter past ten, y'know."

"We're quite ready, Dan. I brought your other mac down. Thought you'd better look a bit decent to take us to the station."

"Right."

Christine went out to the road to watch them go and stood at the gate until the car returned from picking up Mrs. Perkins. As they passed, Dan called, "Shan't be more than an hour, love!" and she gave him a wave of acknowledgment.

One foot on the bottom rung of the gate, her elbows on the top and chin cupped in her hands, she stood for a long while looking at the leaden sky.

Almost a week had passed since Bill died. She could think of him impersonally, remembering him without rancour or regret.

The whole village knew by now of the kindness and consideration Crawford had shown to Mrs. Perkins by his offers of help. They knew, too, that the night before he went away Crawford dined with the Squire.

Christine remembered that night. She had been curled up in a chair with a magazine at Brookfield when the phone rang. It was late—half-past eleven—and she had wondered who could be ringing at that hour. She could tell from the sound of the Squire's voice that he was deeply affected.

"Tell your father Mr. Crawford has decided not to proceed with the scheme. He's agreed to see if we can come to some financial arrangement whereby the rights return to the estate." Lawson-Hope's voice broke a little. "He's a good man—a good man."

She wanted to know more, but he said, "No, no, I must ring the rest of my people who are affected and tell them at once. Tonight."

Phil had told them what the mining engineer had said about the ironstone and the weight his judgment carried with Crawford, but Christine thought there was more to it than that. Bill *had* helped. By dying he had helped. And now he was being taken back to London for burial.

Christine was about to go indoors when she heard the sound of a motor-cycle and craned over the gate, looking down the road. Dick Raymond pulled up close to the gate, but he did not get off his machine.

"Have they gone?"

"Yes."

"Damn. I wanted to try and put things right with Mrs. Perkins."

"Oh, Dick, you're not still worrying?" She was concerned and sympathetic. When he nodded she said,

"But it's so silly. Nobody blames you. Even at the inquest they said it wasn't your fault. It could have happened to anybody."

"But it had to be me who shoved him over."

As he drove away the snow started to fall—big downy flakes that dropped languidly from the skies, spotting the road and hedges and settling unnoticed in her hair. He waved sombrely just before he turned the corner that hid him from view, but long after he was gone she stood there, wondering if he would ever rid his mind from the sense of guilt, wondering just how important to the peace of Ambridge was the shove Dick had given Bill.

XVIII

THE LETTER was lying on the desk in Fairbrother's farm office when Phil came back from market. He read it, turned it over and over in his fingers, sat down and read it again, slowly, deliberately, to make sure he had not misunderstood.

It was formal, correct, brief, the writing firm and the signature neat. There could be no mistaking the contents, but still he examined it, holding it by the corners and twisting it this way and that so the light fell on it from different angles.

"What did you expect? Tearstains and tragedy?"

He started at the sound of Jane's voice behind him and jumped up.

"Jane!" He flourished the letter at her. "What's the meaning of this?"

"I thought it was plain. I'm giving my notice." Her auburn hair was wet with melting snow. "Sorry if I sounded bitter. I didn't mean to be."

He moved across the office towards her, but she opened the old riding mac she was wearing and flapped it vigorously to shake off the snow. He stopped, certain she had done it intentionally to keep him at a distance.

"You really mean to leave?"

"Yes, Phil."

An unwelcome twinge of guilt nagged at him when he saw the sadness in her face.

"What will you do?"

"I'm going home. My people would like to see me

for a while. I—I shall rest for a few weeks before I think about taking another job. Mummy'll be pleased to have me home. She always has a sneaking feeling I'll get into trouble on my own."

The lightness she forced into her manner upset him. He felt he would have preferred her to make a scene, to strike him and abuse him—anything to even up the score between them.

"There'll be lots to do now the scheme's abandoned, Jane."

"Yes, I'm sure there will."

He felt the same helplessness he had known once before as a child. He had been nursing a lamb in his arms—his lamb, the first living thing his father had ever given him to raise. Somehow the lamb sickened and he had watched it die, unable to do anything to save it.

"But you know I must go, Phil," Jane finished simply. Buttoning her mac again, she stood indecisive for a few moments before she buckled her belt. Outside the office the snow, heavier now, covered the fields in a fresh, white blanket. "Pity we can't all wipe the slate clean like that." Her voice was barely above a whisper. "I know how it is, Phil. I've known ever since that night we were out trying to catch the saboteurs."

She made for the door.

"Jane!"

She stopped but did not look round as he moved to her shoulder.

"You're being very sweet, Jane."

"I'm not really!" He could not see her face, could not tell whether she was forcing the cheerfulness she managed to get into her voice. "I'm not a nice person at all. Deep inside I'm full of hates and things—spite, jealousy, everything."

He touched the short damp curls above her collar with his fingers.

"I'll miss you, Jane."

"I hope so—sometimes." She pulled open the door and a flurry of snow slanted into the office and blew across their faces. "I'll—I'll be very upset if you don't!"

He watched her go across the yard.

He would miss her all right. There would be no more of those farming discussions that sharpened their wits; no more companionship in the everyday job of keeping the farm running. . . .

Presently he became aware that Grace was standing beside him, a raincoat slung loosely over her shoulders. Her tracks in the snow, which had muffled the sound of her approach, led from the back door of the house.

He handed Jane's letter to her and turned into the office.

"You had better give it to your father, Grace."

She read it in silence, folded it and slipped it into the pocket of her skirt.

"Will—will it be difficult to replace her?"

Phil shrugged.

"You're sorry she's going." It was more a flat statement than a question.

"Yes," Phil said frankly. "She was a great help."

He took the coat from Grace's shoulders, threw it over a chair and stood before her, looking at the quick rise and fall of her breast, the dark hair framing her delicate small face, the expression of pathetic uncertainty in her eyes.

Shocked to realise he had not looked at her so closely

for months, he allowed his glance to linger over her, caressing the features he had almost forgotten. The determination that had sent him out from Brookfield the previous night, only to falter in the icy fields, came flooding back with the realisation that at last he knew what he wanted. He wanted Grace.

She was in his embrace in a second, trembling against him, crying a little, her arms round him, gripping him fiercely.

"Phil, my darling. Hold me tighter—tighter."

To him the events of the past few months became more remote, fading away into a haze of unreality. Ironstone, sabotage, Bill Slater, even Jane seemed mere disturbing incidents that had momentarily upset the predestined pattern of his life with Grace. He had had things out of proportion. But now the confusion and conflicts of his mind were settled. He could concentrate on realities—the sun, the sweat and the soil—tangible things, like the girl in his arms.

His fingers crept through her neat, black hair, tilting her head back. He kissed her once, gently, full on the lips.

A sudden gust of wind blew a flurry of snow across the floor and slammed the door of the office. In the warm security of his arms she did not start, and, cheek to cheek, rocking gently, they stared out of the window across the snow-covered fields.

He felt at peace. Under that blanket of snow was life, nurtured and tended by past generations of farming folk, land kept in good heart so that he might in his turn reap its rewards for hard work before he, too, passed the heritage to generations yet unborn.

"We'll have a farm of our own," he murmured.

She nodded and nuzzled his neck. Before he went

on he held her away from him a little and tilted her chin so she could look squarely into his serious, grey eyes.

"It'll take time, Grace. I want a farm that I've worked for and earned. If your father helped with money, it wouldn't be the same thing. I want to feel I deserve my land. I—I want to be independent of your father's money——"

"That won't come between us, Phil," she said. "What's money? The only wealth I know is the richness of your love. I've been so poor—so very poor— without it."

"Then you'll wait?"

Her hands stole up around his neck and pulled him down to her glistening lips.

"I'll wait," she whispered.